BABY
ON THE RANCH

BABY
ON THE RANCH

BY

SUSAN MEIER

MILLS
BOON®

First published in Great Britain 2011
by Mills & Boon, an imprint of Harlequin (UK) Limited.
Large Print edition 2011
Harlequin (UK) Limited, Eton House,
18-24 Paradise Road, Richmond, Surrey TW9 1SR

ISBN: 978 0 263 22246 3

Harlequin (UK) policy is to use papers that are natural,
renewable and recyclable products and made from
wood grown in sustainable forests. The logging and
manufacturing process conform to the legal environmental
regulations of the country of origin.

Printed and bound in Great Britain
by CPI Antony Rowe, Chippenham, Wiltshire

CHAPTER ONE

SUZANNE CALDWELL shoved against the spot in the door of the Old West Diner where the Waitress Wanted sign filled the glass. The scent of fresh apple pie greeted her, along with a rush of noise. Though there were no more than ten people at the counter and in the booths, the place was as rowdy as a party. Women wearing jeans and tank tops sat with men dressed in jeans, T-shirts and cowboy hats.

She didn't get two steps into the room before the noise level began to drop. As if noticing the stranger, people stopped talking midsentence.

She clutched her six-month-old baby, Mitzi. There was nothing like walking into a roomful of staring strangers to make you realize how alone you were in the world. And she was definitely alone. She'd run out of gas about a mile out of

Whiskey Springs, Texas, and, literally, had no one to call for help.

No family. Her grandmother had died six months ago and her mom had died when Suzanne was six. Her dad, whoever he was, had never acknowledged her.

Her mom and grandmother were both only children, so she had no aunts, no uncles, no cousins.

And no friends. The wonderful sorority sisters who'd vowed to be her ally for life had dumped her when she got pregnant by a popular university professor. It was her fault, they'd said, and had accused her of trying to ruin Bill Baker's career. As if. The guy had gone on a campaign to seduce her and had wormed his way into her life because of her grandmother's fortune. When Martha Caldwell made some major mistakes in money management and lost the bulk of her wealth, Professor Baker suddenly didn't want to see Suzanne anymore. And he most certainly wanted no part of their baby.

So, yeah. She was alone. Alone. Broke. Desperate to make a home for herself and her baby. And she'd left Atlanta bound for Whiskey Springs, hoping to find some help.

But after walking the last mile on a hot June day, her heels ached in her black stiletto boots. Mitzi squirmed in her arms. Her heavy diaper bag was dislocating her shoulder. Still, she kept her head high as she made her way to the first empty booth. By the time she got there, the diner was dead silent.

A waitress shuffled over. "Help you?"

She cleared her throat. "I'd like a piece of the apple pie I can smell, a cup of coffee, a glass of milk and some pudding, please."

"What kind of pudding?"

She swallowed. Not one person had turned back to his or her coffee or food. They just stared as if she were a zombie or vampire or some other mythical creature they'd never seen before. "What kind do you have?"

"Vanilla or chocolate."

"Mitzi loves vanilla."

Without so much as a word of acknowledgment, the waitress scurried away.

"You're not from around here."

Knowing the man could only be talking to her, she followed the voice and found herself staring into a pair of the shrewdest eyes she'd ever seen. Cool, calculating, so black the pupils were almost invisible, his eyes never blinked, never wavered as they held her gaze.

Toto, we are not in Kansas anymore.

"No, I'm not from around here."

"What's your business?"

"None of yours." She turned away from the penetrating, unsettling eyes and shifted Mitzi on her lap.

To her horror, the man walked over and plopped down on the bench seat across from hers. His full lips pulled upward into a devilish smile. His dark eyes danced with pleasure. "Now, see. That's not just a bad attitude. It's also wrong."

She should have been scared to death. He was big. Not fat, but tall and broad-shouldered. The kind of guy who could snap a little five-foot-five girl like her in two. But instead of fear, a very unladylike shiver of lust rippled down her spine.

"Everything that happens in Whiskey Springs is my business because this is my town."

Not at all happy with herself for even having two seconds of attraction to an ill-mannered stranger, she said, "*Your* town? What are you, the sheriff?"

He chuckled. The people at the counter and in the booths around them also laughed.

"No. I'm Cade Andreas. I own this town. I bought all the buildings last year. I lease the businesses back to their proprietors, but I still own every square inch, including the one you're sitting on."

Oh, good God. *This* was Cade Andreas?

Fear and confusion immediately replaced attraction. Wasn't the Andreas family broke? She owned one-third of Andreas Holdings stock and hadn't been able to sell it because the company was on the skids. What was he doing buying a town?

"And I'd like to know what brings you to my town."

She raised her gaze to his face. A day-old growth of beard covered his chin and cheeks, giving him a sexily disreputable look. His lips were full, firm, kissable. His nose had been broken—undoubtedly in a fight—but it wasn't disfigured, more like masculine. Definitely not dainty. There was nothing dainty about this man. He was all male. One hundred percent, grade A, prime specimen sexy.

Finally, their eyes connected. Her chest tightened. Her breathing stalled. She could have blamed that on her unwitting attraction, but refused. A guy who bought a town had to be more than a little arrogant. Definitely past vain. Maybe even beyond narcissistic. And she'd learned her lesson about narcissistic men with Mitzi's father. It would be a cold, frosty day in hell before she got involved with another self-absorbed man. So she refused to be attracted to Cade Andreas. Refused.

But she still needed a job. She might own stock worth millions of dollars, but nobody wanted to buy it. Potential didn't sell stock these days. Dividends did. And in the past two years Andreas Holdings hadn't paid any. So she was hoping that since she owned one-third of the company they could at least let her work there. The choice to approach Cade Andreas, the youngest of the three brothers who owned controlling interest of Andreas Holdings stock and ran the company, was simply a matter of practicality. Texas was driving distance. New York City, the headquarters for the corporate offices, wasn't. Still, if they gave her a job, she'd get there somehow. She'd go anywhere that she could put down roots and make a home. Maybe find some friends.

"What brings you to my town?"

This time the words were harsh. Not quite angry, but definitely losing patience.

She glanced at the waitress who stood behind the counter, balancing a coffeepot and Suzanne's piece of pie, obviously holding them hostage until she answered Cade.

She looked back at him. His already-sharp eyes had narrowed in displeasure, and she had the sudden, intense intuition that if she told him who she was—in front of his adoring friends and the frozen waitress—he would not jump for joy. She would bet her last dollar that none of these people knew how much trouble Andreas Holdings was in and Cade would not be happy with the person who announced it.

There was no way she could say who she was and why she was here without talking about something he would no doubt want kept private, and no way she could explain her presence in this two-bit town so far from a major highway that no one was ever just passing through.

She glanced around, saw the sign in the door advertising for a waitress and grabbed the first piece of good luck that had come her way in over a year.

"I heard about the job for a waitress, so I came."

"In your fancy boots, with your baby all dolled up?"

"We put on our best stuff," she said, making herself sound as if she fit the part of a waitress. She regretted the deception, but if anybody ever deserved to be played, this guy did. Owned a town, huh? She potentially held the future of his family's company in her hands just by choosing whom to sell her stock to, yet he'd never once considered that she might be somebody worthy of his time. "For the interview."

A short, round dark-haired woman wearing an

apron scampered out of the kitchen. "You're looking for a job?"

"Yes." The truth of that brought her back to reality. Her purpose for coming to Whiskey Springs *had been* to get a job—from Andreas Holdings. Now that plan was on hold. She wasn't exactly here to be a waitress, but money was money. And she needed some. Now. Today. She had enough cash to pay for her piece of pie and even buy extra milk for Mitzi, but after that she and Mitzi were sleeping in her car.

"I'm Suzanne Caldwell." Because her grandmother had held the stock in a trust, her name wasn't mentioned on any documents, so she could give it without worry. "This is my baby, Mitzi."

Mitzi picked that exact moment to cry. The little brunette scrambled over. "I'm Amanda Mae and if you want a job, you've got it." She shot Cade an evil look, causing Suzanne to immediately love her. "Real men don't make babies cry."

Cade held up his hands innocently. "Hey, I was on my own side of the booth the whole time. I didn't touch her."

"You're threatening her mama."

His face fell. "I never threatened her!"

"Just your voice is threatening."

He sighed. "Yeah. Right. Whatever."

She took the baby. "Would you like a bottle, little Mitzi?"

Suzanne said, "I ordered some milk and pudding for her."

Amanda Mae looked horrified. "June Marie, where are you with this baby's food?"

The waitress hustled over, set Suzanne's pie in front of her and poured her a cup of coffee before she rushed away and got both the pudding and the milk.

Eyes narrowed, Cade studied the woman across the booth from him. She was a pretty little package. Eyes so blue they bordered on the purple color of the wildflowers that grew on his pasture in the spring. Black hair cut in a straight, blunt line at her chin, giving her a dramatic look that didn't fit with a woman who needed a job as a waitress. And those boots. Black stilettos. The kind a man envisioned on his chest, pinning him to a bed.

He stopped those thoughts. She might be a pretty with her perfect nose and full, tempting lips, but he wasn't interested.

Still, he had no doubt that he had to keep an eye on her. Something wasn't right with her. It wasn't just her city-girl clothes. Her demeanor didn't fit. Waitresses didn't have smooth hands, perfect posture, an unblinking stare.

He rose from the booth. "Well, seeing as how you seem to have gotten the job you wanted, I guess we'll be running into each other from time to time."

She only smiled. A cool, remote smile that heated his blood and all but challenged him to turn on the charm and see how long it would take to get that smile to thaw. Luckily, he was smarter than that.

Amanda Mae said, "Do you have someplace to stay, honey?"

She faced the diner owner. "I— No. Actually, I need a place to stay."

"Hotel's in the next town over," Cade said, striding back to his seat at the counter and his now-cold coffee.

Amanda Mae shot him another evil glare. "Or she could use the apartment upstairs until she gets on her feet."

"I'd like that." Suzanne pressed her fingers to Amanda Mae's hand in a gesture of appreciation that stopped Cade cold. Maybe she was in need of a little help? Her crisp white blouse and fancy jeans could be the last good things she owned. He hadn't heard a car drive up. He glanced out the big front window into the street. He didn't see a car. She could be dead broke—

Nope. His business sense wouldn't accept that. Something about her screamed money. Big money. If she was pretending she didn't have any, there was a reason.

Damn. He was going to have to keep an eye on her.

Immediately after Cade left, Amanda Mae took Suzanne upstairs to look at the little furnished apartment.

"One of the waitresses always lives here," she

said, leading Suzanne into the tiny bedroom that barely had enough space for a crib and a double bed. "So we keep it furnished."

Gratitude weakened Suzanne's knees. At least they wouldn't have to sleep in her car tonight. She turned to Amanda Mae with a smile. "Thanks. I appreciate it."

Amanda Mae stuffed a few bills into her palm. "And here's some money to go to the secondhand store down the street and buy some sheets and towels."

Her face reddened. This time last year she was telling her grandmother she was three months pregnant and that her baby's daddy wanted no part of her. Her wonderful, loving grandmother had taken her hand and told her not to worry. That everything would be okay. Even though she'd made some bad investments, they still had the Andreas Holdings stock.

A couple of months hadn't just changed everything; they'd taken away her home, her only family. Instead of being a well-loved granddaughter, she was a broke single mom. So alone her only contacts had been lawyers and accountants, until her grandmother's estate was settled. Then even they didn't call.

Tears welled up. She caught Amanda Mae's gaze. "I'll pay you back."

Amanda Mae squeezed her hand. "In good time. For now, I'm just happy to have some help for the breakfast crowd."

Driving back to his ranch, Cade speed-dialed the number for his assistant.

"Hey, Cade."

"Hey, Eric." He'd hired Eric right out of grad school because he was sharp and educated, but also because he had total recall. If someone mentioned an aunt, cousin, sister, brother or long-lost friend even once in a conversation, Eric would remember him or her. "Have you ever heard of Suzanne Caldwell?"

"Can't say that I have."

Damn.

"Who is she?"

"Just a woman who came into the diner today.

She took the waitress job, but something just didn't seem right about her."

"Ah. I'm guessing your business sense kicked up."

He scowled at the phone. "Don't poke fun at my business sense. It's made me rich enough that I'd never have to work another day in my life. While you, on the other hand, still work for me."

He disconnected the call. But when he thought of Suzanne, the hair on his nape snapped up. Damn it! Why would a waitress activate his business sense? And why was he going back to his ranch when his instincts were screaming that he should be checking into this?

Slamming on the brakes, he manipulated his truck through a fishtail and headed back into town. He pulled it into a parking space at the diner, but when he walked by the huge front window, he saw that the new waitress wasn't inside.

His instincts calmed, his intuition quieted and he cursed himself for being the suspicious fool that Eric hinted he was. But before he could turn around and go back to his truck, he saw Suzanne coming down the outside steps from the second-floor apartment, carrying her baby.

A hot rush of desire whooshed through him. Luckily, the hair on his nape also prickled the way it always did right before a negotiation went sour. The first reaction might have been attraction. But the nape prickle? That was what told him he was about to get into a fight. Not a fistfight, but a disagreement, or maybe a battle to protect what was his. He slid into the alley between the general store and the hardware and watched her head up the street.

Unfortunately, the view from behind was every bit as stunning as her front profile. Her straight black hair fringed the collar of the crisp white blouse that hugged a trim, toned back. It slid along the indent of her small waist to an absolutely perfect behind that swayed ever so slightly with every step of her long legs—legs made to look longer and sexier by her stiletto boots.

Attraction hit him like a warm ocean wave and left him drowning in sensation. This time he had to admit it was only attraction. He tried to blink it away but failed. There was just so much about her that was geared to appeal to a man. No male alive could resist that kind of shapely body. Especially when the pretty little package had a face to match. Dramatic hair. Eyes that could very well glow in the dark.

He shook his head to clear the haze. Fantasizing would not do either one of them any good. He needed to figure out why she set off his business alarms or it would drive him crazy. Yes, that might make him a control freak. But he was a rich, successful control freak. And if his business sense said jump, his answer was always how high.

When he was sure she was far enough ahead that she wouldn't see him, he followed her. When she ducked into the secondhand store, he stopped. He waited for her to get deep enough into the building that she wouldn't notice him hovering beyond the display in the big glass front window.

Judy Petrovic, proprietor of Yesterday's Goods, ambled over to her.

Suzanne turned and offered her a sweet, sincere smile, which nearly knocked Cade off his feet. He'd never seen her smile. Well, he'd seen her sassy imitation smile, but never a genuine smile until now. And he was glad. Had she smiled at him like that in the diner he worried he would have stuttered.

She handed her baby to Judy, then her heavy-looking diaper bag. Judy bounced the little girl as Suzanne dipped down and rummaged through a table of what looked to be sheets, maybe towels. Walking back and forth from the display to the cash register, she made a pile of linens before she grabbed a pair of secondhand jeans and a T-shirt, and several things for her baby. After Judy rang up her purchases, she paid with crumpled-up bills that she'd been clutching in her left hand.

Cade pulled back and slid around to the side of the building, his chest tightening with regret. She'd said she'd come to Whiskey Springs for the job as a waitress and she'd asked for it without a hint of regret. Now she was buying somebody's old, worn sheets to fit on the old, worn mattress on a bed that had seen more years than most of the people in this town.

She really was broke.

And here he was spying on her like some old goof.

He was a goof. The truth was he wasn't entirely sure that his sixth sense about her really was his business sense. It could be nothing but attraction. Lord knew it had been so long since he'd been naturally overwhelmingly attracted to a woman that he might have forgotten the signs. He'd botched his first marriage so much that he stayed away from any woman who might inspire anything more than lust. And a woman with a baby wasn't somebody a man should be fooling around with. Since he didn't want to be attracted to Suzanne, he could be trying to kid himself into thinking it was his sixth sense. Rationalizing so he didn't have to admit to anybody that he virtually tripped over his tongue when he looked at her.

A dry dusty breeze swirled around him, reminding him that he was hiding in an alley, spying on a waitress.

Good God. What was he doing?

CHAPTER TWO

CADE raised his arm to wave hello, but it slid across silk sheets, and the wonderful dream he was having burst like a bubble.

He bounced up in bed and scrubbed his hand across his mouth. It was the same dream he always had. It began with him riding up to the main corral, watching his deceased wife, Ashley, as she tended the long strip of flowers she'd planted along the road to the barns, stables and corrals. No matter how many times he'd told her that barns did not need flower beds, he'd never been able to get it through her head.

But when he had the dream, the chance to see her, he didn't want to argue about flowers. Even in sleep, his heart knocked against his ribs, and he wanted to hold her, to kiss her, to tell her how much he missed her.

He squeezed his eyes shut. He didn't get the chance to do any of those. Just like always, he hadn't even gotten to say hello. His subconscious wouldn't even give him hello, forget about a hug, a light kiss.…

Knowing he couldn't give in to the sadness, he tossed back the covers and headed for the shower. He'd gotten beyond losing Ashley. She'd died two years ago and he wasn't an idiot. She was gone. He couldn't deny that there was a hole in his chest where his heart should have been, but that part of his life was over.

He ducked his head under the spray and let the water beat down on him, remind him he was real, remind him he had satisfying work, a huge ranch, oil wells, a town that depended on him. There wasn't a man in the state of Texas more fulfilled than he was.

It was enough.

He shoved his legs into jeans, wrestled a T-shirt over his head and jogged downstairs. Though it was only 4:00 a.m., Mrs. Granger, the cook, would have coffee in the kitchen. Still, he didn't turn toward the warm scent. He also didn't go to his office. It was hours before the New York Stock Exchange opened, so there was no point going to his desk. Instead, he found an old pair of boots, jumped in his truck and headed for the stables.

That was what he usually did after the dream. Not just because he needed something to occupy his mind, but because the dream left him hungry, angry, and he wouldn't inflict himself on any-body until he settled down.

He hadn't expected lights to be on in the long red stable, but he wasn't surprised to see his fore-man and father-in-law, Jim Malloy, cloistered in his office.

"What are you doing up so early?"

Jim's chair creaked as he leaned back. "Me? This is my normal starting time. My guys will be here in an hour or so. I need to get caught up on paperwork. Better question is what are you doing up so early? Stock exchange doesn't open for hours."

He flopped to the chair in front of Jim's desk. Shrugged.

"You had that dream again."

Cade said nothing.

"Pain's probably never going to go away."

"I'm fine. I have my work."

"A lot of work," Jim said with a laugh.

They were quiet for a few seconds then Jim rose. "Coffee?"

"Is it fresh?"

"Come on. I haven't been here *that* long. Of course it's fresh."

"Then I'll have some."

Jim poured two mugs of coffee and handed Cade's to him before he sat on the edge of the desk. "You were a good husband to Ashley and you're still a good son-in-law."

Cade snorted in derision. His father-in-law had known about the time Cade had spent away from Ashley. The times business had taken him to other cities for weeks at a clip. It was kind of him to tell Cade he'd been a good husband, but Cade wasn't so easily buffaloed.

Jim patted his knee. "You *were* a good husband. Just because you don't get to talk to Ashley in your dream, it doesn't mean you're being punished."

Jim was wrong again. He'd been out of town the day Ashley died. Not with her. Not holding her hand, but sweet-talking an oil baron into selling his company. And Ashley had died alone. That, he believed, was what his subconscious was telling him every damn time he had the dream. Just as she hadn't gotten to say goodbye to him, his subconscious wouldn't let him say goodbye to her. Not even symbolically.

Still, he didn't argue with Jim. He took a sip of coffee then choked it out. "My God. Sludge tastes better than this."

"Oh, yeah? And when, exactly, have you tasted sludge?"

Cade laughed. Jim went back to his seat behind the desk. They occupied themselves talking foals and fences, the price of beef and which animals they'd breed. Seconds turned to minutes and minutes to an hour and with every tick of the clock, the tightness in Cade's chest loosened. The residual sadness from the dream receded. He'd never get a chance to say goodbye to Ashley. He had to accept that and move on.

* * *

Suzanne woke a little after five o'clock and actually showered before Mitzi even stirred. She dressed quickly in the little pink uniform Amanda Mae had given her for her first day as a waitress, then just as quickly dressed Mitzi. She grabbed her cereal and a fresh bottle on her way out the apartment door.

As expected, she found Amanda Mae in the diner kitchen, kneading a batch of bread.

"Make room on the prep table for me," she said, sliding Mitzi into the seat of the swing they'd set up in the corner. She and Amanda Mae had already decided Mitzi could be in the diner with Suzanne while she worked. When the diner got busy and the kitchen heated from all the cooking, they could move the swing and Mitzi to the little alcove between the dining room and kitchen. But now, the kitchen was a quiet, homey place, suitable for a baby.

"As soon as I feed Mitzi, I'm going to bake a batch of my grandmother's cinnamon rolls."

Amanda Mae's eye brows rose. "Oh, yeah?"

"It's my way of saying thank you for giving me a job."

"Hey, it's no skin off my nose. I know you're probably only temporary, but I need the help. I'm happy for any amount of time you can give me."

Even though Amanda Mae understood, guilt took up residence in Suzanne's chest. She had no idea how things would turn out when she actually spoke with the Andreas brothers about her shares of stock, but she hoped they'd give her a job. She needed to make a home for her baby and waitress pay wasn't as good as working for a shipping conglomerate.

So she fought through the guilt. Not only would she give Amanda Mae a good day's work every day she waitressed, but she'd found a tangible way to pay her back for her kindnesses. The Caldwell cinnamon roll recipe was a family secret, passed down from one Caldwell woman to the next. It was an honor to have it. But it was an even bigger joy to actually eat the cinnamon rolls.

She thought of Cade, hoping a good cinnamon roll might mellow him out, so she could confess who she was on day one of her charade as waitress. Then he could confess that his family didn't have the money to buy her out. So that she could ask for a job before Amanda Mae got accustomed to having her here. It was a long shot. But right now it was all she had.

When Mitzi was fed, she walked around the kitchen gathering the ingredients for the cinnamon rolls. Amanda Mae made room on the prep table for Suzanne and she went to work.

She began with warm water and yeast. When the yeast was ready, she added the other ingredients until she had a nice dough. As the dough rose, the first customers of the morning filtered in and back out again. But while the rolls were baking, the customers in the dining room began asking what was filling the air with the wonderful scent. Some waited long after they'd finished their breakfasts just to get one of the first rolls as they came out of the oven. By seven-thirty, over half were gone.

"Good Lord, girl," Amanda Mae said, staring at the second empty cinnamon roll tray. "We could sell three dozen of these a day."

"People will tire of them," Suzanne said, dusting her hands on her apron before she lifted Mitzi from the swing. She'd just finished putting the last pan into the oven.

"I'm not so sure."

Suzanne worried her bottom lip. "So you think they're good enough to soften a grouchy guy?"

Amanda Mae laughed. "Maybe. But if I were you, I'd try being nice to Cade instead of sniping at him the way you did yesterday."

"You noticed."

"Honey, two polecats fighting over table scraps make fewer sparks."

She winced. "I just don't know what it is about him, but he brings out the worst in me."

Amanda Mae laughed. "Or the best."

"Oh, come on. You're not saying we're attracted."

"Stranger things have happened."

"I can't be attracted to him."

"Figured as much. Figured you've got business with him. The only reason city slickers come to Whiskey Springs is because they have business with Cade."

She sucked in a breath. "I do."

"Then forget all about your hormones and be nice to the guy. At least until you get a chance to tell him what you need."

A little after eight, Cade was lost in work and didn't hear Eric come into the room until he said, "Have you even had coffee yet?"

Pulling away from the computer, he stretched his arms above his head and glanced at the clock.

"If you call the sip of the sludge I had in Jim's office coffee, then yes. But if you're talking about real coffee. No. I haven't even been to the kitchen yet. Did you get some?"

Eric waved a tall mug. "My first stop is always for coffee. But if you want, I can go back and get a cup for you, too."

He leaned back in his chair. "I'm fine."

Eric sat on one of the two chairs in front of Cade's desk. "So did you find out anything interesting yesterday from Suzanne Caldwell?"

He'd forgotten all about the waitress he'd met the day before. But now that Eric mentioned her, he was back to being curious again. She was too pretty, too sophisticated, too coolly elegant to be a real waitress.

Glad to have his mind off his failure as a husband, he rose from his desk and began to pace. "The thing is I have no idea how she got into town since she didn't have a car. Plus, she didn't have any luggage. Even a poor woman would have had luggage, if only one suitcase." He faced Eric again. "She could be running from something. Or someone. And that could be trouble."

"If this woman worries you so much why not go into the diner for breakfast? Maybe you can get some answers by turning on the charm."

The last thing he wanted to do was turn on the charm. He was way too attracted to her to tempt fate. Still, he didn't like people who kept secrets. His whole town was an open book. Everybody knew everybody else and they liked it that way. He couldn't tolerate somebody coming in and stirring up the pot.

That in and of itself was reason enough that he probably should try to cuddle up to her a little. Show her he was a nice guy. A great guy. And maybe she'd tell him her story?

Convinced this was the right thing to do, he gave Eric enough work to keep him busy for the morning and jumped into his truck. He slid it into an empty parking space on Main Street and shut down the ignition. Oddly, he peered into the rearview mirror and checked his hair, which was sticking up on one side. He patted it down then scowled at himself.

What was he doing? He wasn't here to ask her on a date. He didn't want a date. He wanted information.

He rammed the truck door to open it and all but stormed into the diner. And there she stood. Order pad in hand. Pencil behind her ear. Crisp white apron covering the pink candy-striped waitress uniform Amanda Mae insisted that all her girls wear.

As the little bell above the door tinkled announcing his arrival, she glanced over at him. Their gazes caught. Her pretty violet eyes widened and his heart flip-flopped.

He held back a curse. Hadn't he already gone over all of this in his head? He'd had the love of his life, and he'd botched that relationship. So he wasn't interested in trying again. And even if he was looking for a fling, something discreet and purely for sex, Suzanne Caldwell was not the woman he would choose. She might be pretty. Very pretty. *Dramatically* pretty. But she had a baby and he was certain she was holding back information about herself. He was not interested, except to make sure she wasn't a threat to the peace of his people.

He ambled to the counter, slapped Marty Higgins on the back and sat on the stool next to him. "Morning, Marty."

"Morning, Cade."

He and Marty were the only two patrons left from the morning rush, but that might be good. In a quiet diner, the waitresses sometimes had nothing better to do than talk to the customers.

As casually as possible, he slid his gaze to Suzanne's again. "Morning, Ms. Caldwell."

"Good morning, Mr. Andreas."

"It's Cade," Marty corrected before he took a sip of his coffee.

Cade pulled out his most charming smile. "He's right. Everybody calls me Cade."

"Is that an order?"

His eyes narrowed. "It's not an order and it's also not a reason for you to be so prickly. Especially when I haven't even had coffee yet."

She pulled the pencil from behind her ear. "So you want a coffee."

"And eggs over easy, bacon, home fries, rye toast and two blueberry pancakes."

She stopped writing and glanced at him again. Her gaze rippled from his face down his chest and probably would have gone the whole way to his toes had he been standing.

"You got a problem?"

"You're awfully fit for a guy who eats like a horse."

Hormones bubbled up in him. He had always been proud that he was in shape as a result of hard work, not some sissy gym. But he didn't like the way his gut tightened or his hormones awoke like a bunch of cowboys at the scent of morning coffee. "Believe me. I'll use it all up before noon." He made a quick shooing motion with his hand. "Just go get it."

She smiled sweetly. "No reason to be prickly."

His hormones spiked. Damn she was sassy!

She turned and sauntered away and he watched every sway of her hips, cursing himself in his head for not looking away as he should have.

"She is a pretty little filly, isn't she?" Marty whispered, leaning in so only Cade could hear.

"Yeah, but she's pretty like a cactus. Nice to look at but a man had better not touch."

Marty chuckled. "See, now I hadn't even gotten to the thinking-about-touching stage. You must have it bad. Especially if you're coming into the diner for breakfast when you've got a damn fine cook at your ranch."

Cade glowered at Marty. "I'm here for information." He stopped himself. Why was he explaining himself to the guy who ran the hardware? Since when did he explain himself to anybody?

Marty slapped a five-dollar bill on the counter and rose. Leaning across toward the kitchen, he yelled, "See you tomorrow, Amanda Mae." He smiled at Suzanne. "You too, sugar."

Suzanne strolled back to the counter, pot of coffee in one hand, cup and saucer in the other.

Placing them in front of Cade, she addressed Marty, "You leave me a halfway decent tip?"

Marty laughed. "Yep."

"Okay, then, you can go."

Marty left, chuckling to himself and shaking his head. Cade's blood pressure rose. The woman knew she could wrap most men around her little finger because of her looks alone. Well, he was not going to be so easy to manipulate as old Marty.

"Cream?"

"No. I drink my coffee black."

"Wow. Alert the media."

She turned to go, but he snagged her wrist. His fingers wrapped around skin so soft they felt pillowed by it. Her scent drifted over to him. Her gaze swung to his.

He fought the urge to swallow. Her eyes were so beautiful it was enough to stop a man's heart. But he was stronger than this. Smarter than to get caught in a woman's web. And he was also a man on a mission. Figure out who she was so he could get rid of her or just get rid of these odd feelings he had every time he was with her.

"How the hell did you ever succeed as a waitress with that attitude?"

She smiled sweetly. "Maybe I didn't? Maybe that's why I had to travel the whole way here to be able to find someone who'd hire me?"

It was the first thing she'd said to him that made perfect sense. He dropped her wrist and let her go. She returned a few minutes later with his food.

Just then her baby let out with a squawk. Seated in a swing set up in the alcove between the dining room and the kitchen, she slapped a rattle against the white tray.

Cade wasn't surprised that her baby was there. Whiskey Springs was a very laid-back town and Amanda Mae was a very sweet, helpful employer. But it had been so long since he'd seen a baby that curiosity overwhelmed him. Gino, his third half brother, had been six months old when their father had died and passed off Gino's care to the adult Andreas sons. But in the eighteen months that had passed, Gino had become a two-year-old, a toddler. He wasn't a baby anymore.

He peeked at the little girl with her big blue

eyes and shiny black hair just like her mother's, and an achy pain circled his heart. Because he had black hair and Ashley had had blue eyes, he'd always imagined that at least one of their kids would have dark hair and Ashley's pale blue eyes. But he and Ashley couldn't have kids.

The reminder made his heart hurt a little more. Not only would he spend the rest of his years without the woman he adored, but also he'd never have kids. Being a father had been the one goal in life he'd wanted more than success. His own father had been a poor excuse for a dad and Cade knew in his heart he could do better. Lots better. If only because he knew exactly what a kid longed for from a father, because he hadn't had it.

He studied the little girl. Her plump cheeks. The spit bubbles she blew as she sputtered and chattered, trying to form words. She was so cute. So happy.

She *was* happy. That had to mean Suzanne was a good mom. But that only brought him back to the same question. Why would a single mom take her baby so far from home for a job that barely paid minimum wage?

When Suzanne walked back to refill his coffee, he caught her hand again. "What are you doing here, really?"

"Maybe I'm running?"

Cade scowled. Now she was teasing him.

But she sighed and said, "Look, I'm not trying to hide my past. It's just kind of embarrassing. I got involved with a college professor who took advantage of my innocence. I was a bit of a starstuck puppy."

Surprised by her easy admission, he leaned back and felt a tad foolish for constantly questioning her motives.

"When I told him I was pregnant, he told me he didn't want anything to do with me or our baby. Eventually I had to quit school. Then my grandmother died and now I'm alone and broke."

Foolishness morphed into regret. His father, the great Stephone Andreas, had done the same thing to his mom—and him. Stephone had gotten his mom pregnant then barely acknowledged Cade's existence until he was eighteen. Then he'd sent a lawyer to offer the trust fund that became Cade's grubstake to make himself a very rich man. But through his entire childhood, his mom had busted her butt to make a life for them. He had a soft spot for single moms.

So why did he continually harass this one?

But before he could apologize, Suzanne caught his gaze and very quietly said, "Where I come from, people share. I just told you my big embarrassing secret. Seems to me you should reciprocate by telling me yours."

Any bit of sympathy he had for her disappeared and was replaced by a swell of annoyance. His biggest life secret was that he'd never gotten the chance to say goodbye to his wife. And that was none of Suzanne's business. Especially since he found her attractive. Ashley was the love of his life. She was a sweet, wonderful woman who would have never talked to him—to anyone— the way Suzanne just had, nosing into personal business.

"Hey, Cade!"

To Cade's complete horror, his mother, Virginia Brown—Ginny for short—walked into the diner and over to him. A tall brunette with sharp green eyes and a perpetual grin on her face, she took the seat Marty had just vacated.

"What are you doing here? Don't you have a cook?"

"Yes, I have a cook." He faced his mother with a warning glare.

She only laughed. "So why are you at the diner?"

She asked the question as Suzanne wiped down the counter in front of them, cleaning away Marty's crumbs. Cade didn't have to reply because Suzanne said, "What can I get for you?"

His mother smiled, but she sniffed the air. "What is that wonderful smell?"

Suzanne straightened with pride. "Cinnamon rolls. I gave Amanda Mae my grandmother's recipe as a thank-you for hiring me."

Even as Suzanne spoke, Cade picked up on the scent himself. Because it had mixed in with the aromas of coffee and pancakes, he'd almost missed it. But the second he homed in on it, his mouth watered.

"I showed her how to make them this morning."

"Are there any left?" Ginny asked hopefully.

Suzanne shrugged. "Maybe a dozen or so."

"I'll have one of those and a cup of coffee."

Cade said, "And I'll have one to go."

Suzanne suddenly became very busy dusting a napkin holder. "Want another cup of coffee?"

"Yeah."

As Suzanne walked away, Ginny burst out laughing. "You don't have to answer my question about why you're here. I think I figured it out on my own."

"You figured wrong."

Ginny laughed again. "Really? Did you miss how she blushed when you said you wanted a cinnamon roll? I think she thinks the way to your heart is through your stomach."

With a deep breath for patience, he faced his mother again. Rolling his eyes in Suzanne's direction to let his mom know he couldn't talk in front of the new waitress, he said, "You've got it all wrong."

She laughed. "Really? You're here when you shouldn't be and she's serving up old family recipes? If you don't see the signs in that then you're the one who's got it all wrong."

Suzanne didn't really hear the exchange, though she caught enough of it to ascertain that the woman sitting next to Cade was his mother. There wasn't much family resemblance. His hair was black. His mother's sable. His eyes were dark. His mother's pale. Their only common trait was that they were both tall and fit.

In his gray T-shirt and tight jeans, Cade looked especially fit. And that was why Suzanne had been thrown off her game and forgot to be nice to him when she waited on him. But she'd tried to rectify that by telling him about Mitzi. She'd even tried to get him to tell her about himself, hoping for an opening to explain she was the owner of the trust that held one-third of his family's company's stock.

But he hadn't bitten and now he wasn't alone at the counter anymore. Worse, he was taking his cinnamon roll out. He wouldn't eat it in the diner, swoon with ecstasy and be open to anything she told him. By the time he ate the thing, he could even forget who'd made it. She needed to come clean with him about who she was. If she could just get fifteen minutes of his time, in private, she could end this blasted charade.

One cinnamon roll in a take-out box and another on a dessert plate for Cade's mom, she walked over to the counter, poured Cade's mom's coffee and set a cinnamon roll in front of her. As she set Cade's take-out box in front of him, his mom very sweetly said, "I didn't catch your name."

Hoping to get him to stay, Suzanne refilled Cade's cup. "It's Suzanne. Suzanne Caldwell."

"I'm Ginny Brown. I used to be the town librarian, but since my son struck it rich, I now own the bookstore."

As Suzanne said, "It's nice to meet you," she noticed the burn of embarrassment crawl up Cade's neck to his face.

Ginny patted his arm. "He hates it when I mention his being rich."

Cade caught her gaze as if pleading for mercy, a move so unexpected that something soft and warm cradled Suzanne's heart. It was sweet that he couldn't be angry with his mom. But it was also curious that Ginny believed he was still rich.

Unless even she didn't know about the Andreas Holdings troubles?

Cautious, she ran the damp cloth along the counter again. "You should be happy your mom is proud of you."

"There's such a thing as being too proud."

She shrugged. "Maybe. But I think I would have liked to have known what that felt like. My mom died when I was six."

Ginny gasped. "I'm so sorry."

She shrugged again. "I had a good grandmother to raise me." Even as she said that, she glanced back at the kitchen. In a lot of ways Amanda Mae reminded her of her grandmother. Except younger. Probably about her mom's age. Ever since she'd arrived the day before, Amanda Mae had been nothing but kind. This morning's customers had accepted her, as well. And she liked them. If she didn't have other business to attend to, this would be a perfect place to make home.

But she did have other business.

She faced Cade and his mom. "Anyway, it's from my gram that I learned how to make the cinnamon rolls."

"Well, if they taste as good as they smell, the people of this town are going to love you forever."

Warmth filled her heart at the possibility. Wouldn't it be nice to have a whole town of friends?

Finished with his breakfast, Cade rose. He tossed a twenty-dollar bill on the counter and picked up his take-out container. "This should cover it and the tip."

With that he left, and she'd missed her chance to tell him who she was.

After about thirty seconds of staring at the door, Suzanne realized she'd watched him go. What female over the age of fifteen wouldn't? He had a strong, broad back, exquisitely outlined by his tight gray T-shirt. And a perfect backside in well-worn jeans. Add boots and a Stetson to that combo and the mouths of women in three states were probably watering right now.

"Could I have some more coffee?"

Shaking herself out of her daze, Suzanne smiled down at Cade's mother only to see that Ginny was smiling up at her. Shrewdly. Craftily.

"You know, we're having a party at Cade's ranch on Saturday night. I'd love it if you'd come."

CHAPTER THREE

BECAUSE Cade didn't venture into the diner the rest of the week, Suzanne knew she had to go to his party.

She had Amanda Mae drive her to her car to get her two suitcases on Saturday afternoon. The diner owner's eyebrows rose when she saw the powder blue Mercedes, but she said nothing. In the four days they'd worked together, an odd kind of bond had grown between the two women. Since her grandmother's death, Suzanne had felt alone, adrift, and she sensed Amanda Mae didn't often get close to people, either.

But though their growing friendship bolstered Suzanne's courage enough that she knew she could talk to Cade that night, she also realized that she was growing attached to Amanda Mae. If she stayed much longer and got a job at Andreas Holdings, she'd have to move away.

Then she'd feel a real loss and so would Amanda Mae. Tonight had to be the night she talked to Cade.

That evening she dressed in the only cocktail dress she'd kept—a little red sheath—her grandmother's pearls and red stiletto sandals. When Amanda Mai's sixteen-year-old neice, Gloria, arrived to babysit, she gave detailed instructions on caring for Mitzi, then carefully guided herself down the outside stairway in the waning light.

Using the directions Amanda Mae had written out for her, she confidently drove to Cade's ranch. But maneuvering down the long lane that led to his house, she was so confused she nearly stopped her car. Though the house was huge, it was simple. Plain white with black shutters and a black front door with a silver door knocker. There was no valet parking. Cars had just stopped on each side of the lane, but even more cars had been parked in the grass of what should have been his front yard.

She frowned. This was different.

As she opened her car door, music greeted her, making her think the party was outside. Which was fine. She liked garden parties. She especially loved a gorgeous sit-down dinner outside in the early evening. The only problem was an outdoor party sort of screwed up her plan. Because she knew she had to tell Cade who she was, she'd decided to ask him for a few minutes alone. She'd envisioned him saying yes, then herself leading him to his office, where she'd explain who she was in that businesslike environment behind closed doors. First, so no one could overhear. Second, so his reaction would be more professional than personal.

She walked up the cobblestone sidewalk to the front door and rang the bell. But after two minutes and two more bell rings, no one had answered. She tried the silver knocker but that brought no one to the door, either.

With a sigh, she walked around the side of the house. If they were outside, she would just join them.

But when she rounded the corner, she stopped dead in her tracks. Long buffet tables were piled high with food. The music she'd heard was a country band playing a square dance. Couples moved around in a circle under the canopy of a gazebo. Lights circled a swimming pool where kids and teenagers were actually swimming. There were no lily pads decorating the pretty blue water. No careful row of flower pots strategically placed to preclude anyone getting to close to the edge. Nope. This pool was in use.

The urge to turn and run enveloped her, but before she could move, Cade's mom hurried over. "Suzanne! You look exquisite."

"Thanks." She took in Ginny's jeans and bright yellow T-shirt, her cowboy boots. "I didn't realize this was a—"

"Barbecue." Ginny winced. "Sorry. I just assumed you'd realize that in Texas *party* usually means *barbecue.*"

Cade picked that precise second to walk over. Dressed in jeans and a chambray shirt with a bolo tie and a Stetson, he looked like a man who could own a town. Sleek, sexy, sharp and just country enough to remind a woman she was on his turf.

The crackle of attraction that raced through her competed with a rumble of warning. *Tell him.*

Get him alone and tell him who you are. Do not waste another second.

Before she could utter a peep, though, Cade's eyes made a quick sweep from her sandaled feet up her dress to the top of her head and sent another burst of attraction through her.

He smiled slyly. "Come on. Surely you knew this was a barbecue. Everybody in the other forty-nine states knows barbecue is Texas's middle name."

But Cade wasn't one bit sorry she hadn't dressed for a barbecue. Her sexy little sheath was just short enough to show off her great legs. Her super-high-heel sandals sent the blood humming through his veins. The pearls gave her a classy, elegant look.

What if she'd dressed like this deliberately? Wanting him to notice her?

"Let me introduce you around before dinner." Ginny took Suzanne's arm and turned her to the crowd. "You've met most of these people at the diner. Still, there are a few you haven't."

"But I—" Suzanne protested, but it was as if

his mom didn't hear. And just like that, Suzanne had been spirited away.

He watched them go. His eyes narrowed as his gaze honed in on the back—or should he say lack of back—in Suzanne's dress. It was literally open from her neck to her hips…another inch and it would have been illegal in some states.

But it wasn't. It was simply mind-numbingly sexy.

Eyes narrowed, he watched as his mother introduced her to Jeb and Caroline Hunter, the couple who owned the ranch next to his. She smiled politely and shook hands with Jeb, but her gaze wandered over to his.

Before he had a chance to react, his mom took her to Tom Calhoun, Bruce Murphy, Danny Jones and Joshua Turner. All four were recent university graduates. Tom worked at the bank with his father. Bruce had taken over the local car repair shop. Josh was a freelance certified public accountant and Danny was still looking for a job.

He stiffened a bit. Any one of those men was

more suited to her. They were her age. Just starting out like she was.

But, once again, after shaking hands, Suzanne's
gaze ambled back to his.

He smiled. Well. Well. Maybe she wasn't interested in men her own age? And maybe he'd
been playing this all wrong. She might have a
baby, but she'd been burned by that child's daddy.
Maybe she wasn't interested in another long-
term relationship? Maybe she wasn't interested
in a relationship at all? Maybe she was a young,
healthy, sexy woman looking for a little fun, a
little romance.

And from the way her gaze kept streaming
back to his, maybe she was looking for that fun
with him?

His eyes never left her as his mother trotted
her through the group, introducing her to all the
guests. Even the kids in the pool. But every few
seconds, her gaze would wander back to his and
he'd smile.

Until finally, *finally,* his mother got her a glass
of wine from a passing waiter and left her with
Missy Jo Johnson and Amanda Mae. This time,

when her gaze ambled over to his, he nudged his head to indicate she should break away, come to him.

It was a test. If she came over, he'd know she was interested. If she didn't…well, he had other guests to pursue.

Just as he expected, she excused herself and walked over.

Playing with her pearls, she cleared her throat. "Um, Cade, could you and I go somewhere private to talk?"

Sweet success sparked through him. He didn't mind leaving the party. His guests were entertained and probably no one would miss him. More important, no one would be so foolhardy as to come looking for him.

She glanced up at him hopefully.

He smiled down at her. In ten minutes the charcoal beneath the beef wouldn't be the only thing sizzling.

"Sure, sugar."

With his hand at the small of her back, he guided her through the French doors into the formal dining room. The velvet skin of her back tickled his palm with every step she made. Little beads of sweat formed on the back of his neck.

She peeked back at him. "Do you have a den?"

"Den?"

"You know, sort of an office. Someplace private?"

He'd intended to simply take her to his bed. But he wasn't about to argue over logistics. In the marble-tile foyer with the huge crystal chandelier, he pointed straight ahead. He let her get a few steps in front of him so he could take in the view of her gorgeous back, her nicely rounded bottom caressed by the soft material of her perfect red dress. He pressed his hand to his chest to still his beating heart. She was absolutely perfect.

Whoever said money didn't buy happiness was a complete liar.

"Second door down."

She stepped into the room ahead of him. He closed the door and locked it.

Apparently hearing the click, she turned and frowned at him. "You're locking the door?"

"Well, you don't want to get caught do you?"

She frowned. Her full lips turned down prettily,

creating a dimple in her right cheek. Cade all but rubbed his hands together with glee.

"No. I don't."

She sipped her wine. Realizing she might be nervous, he didn't immediately pounce, but ambled to the bar and poured himself two fingers of Scotch. They might have to get back to the party, but the beef wouldn't be done for another hour. They had plenty of time.

He motioned to the black leather sofa. "Seat?"

She smiled nervously. "I think I'd rather stand."

His brow puckered. Confusion eclipsed the heat sparking in his blood stream.

"I…um…" She glanced down at her wine, then back up at him with a hesitant smile. "Well, there's something that I have to tell you."

That didn't quite compute. "Tell me?"

"Yes." She sucked in a breath. "I'm Suzanne Caldwell."

His eyes narrowed.

"You don't recognize the name because my grandmother never had her name on any documents. She held everything in trust."

His hormones stilled. "Held what in trust?"

She cleared her throat. Swallowed again. "The one-third interest in Andreas Holdings that your father had given her."

His hormones died. His muscles tensed and his brain went to red alert.

"*You're* the missing shareholder?"

She nodded.

Cade swayed a bit, downed his Scotch and fought the urge to fall to the sofa. "Well, this is a hell of a time to tell me."

"I couldn't think of a better time—or way. The times I saw you in the diner there were people around. I know your father's company has fallen in hard times because I couldn't sell my shares—"

His face fell in horror. "You tried to sell your shares?"

"What else was I to do? My grandmother's estate—furniture, art, everything—went to pay off debts I didn't realize Gram was accumulating. I have no money."

"At least there's one thing you weren't lying about."

She gaped at him. "I never lied at all! I told you the truth. I had come here to Whiskey

Springs looking for a job. In fact, that's why I'm here right now."

"You want a job?"

"Why not? I own one-third of the company. Surely, there's something I can do at Andreas Holdings. Something that pays enough that I can support my baby."

He squeezed his eyes shut, counted to a hundred and still couldn't control his temper. He didn't know who he was more angry with, her for not telling him who she was the day she arrived, or himself for being such an idiot. Attracted to the enemy. Because that's what she was. Whether she knew it or not, she held more shares of his father's company than any of the Andreas brothers. Yes, united they owned controlling interest, but if they ever had a fight or came down on different sides of an issue with the company, *she'd* rule.

They needed to get those shares back. But even though he could afford to buy her out, his brothers couldn't. They were rich but didn't have that kind of money to spare. And he wouldn't buy her shares because, added to his own, they'd give him controlling interest. Then he and his brothers wouldn't be equals anymore. As it stood, everybody knew he had about ten times the money his brothers had. But when it came to owning their family's company, they were all equals. His buying her out would ruin that.

He took off his Stetson and tossed it across the room.

"I need time to think."

"To me there's nothing to think about. I need a job. I own one-third of a company. It's a no-brainer."

"No, it isn't. The company isn't here. It's headquartered in New York."

"So you're telling me you can't give me a job?"

No. He was stalling for time, trying to figure out how to arrange this so her stock didn't ruin the relationship that had finally been forged between the four Andreas half brothers.

He glanced over at her pretty, pouty expression and his hormones jumped again. This was so not how he'd expected to be spending the next hour.

"Do you have any skills?"

"I was an art history major. One semester away from getting a degree."

He groaned. Like Darius had any use for an art history major.

"My brothers are going to kill me."

She walked over, stood directly in front of him. The scent of her cologne combined with the shear force of her femininity and sent his hormones scurrying to life again.

"Why? I'm the owner of the stock, not you."

He scrubbed his hand across his mouth. "Greeks have a long tradition of killing messengers."

She laughed and he fought the urge to squeeze his eyes shut. He needed twenty minutes alone to think this through, but he couldn't send her back to the party unescorted. God only knew what she'd tell his guests.

"All right." He strode around the desk and flopped into the tall-back black leather chair. Whether he liked it or not, he could not make this decision alone. He pointed at the captain's chairs in front of his desk. "Sit."

She ambled to the desk. "What are we doing?"

"We're calling my brother."

"Ah."

Ah? Even the way she'd said that was cute. Sexy. He had to get rid of her. This was what he got for sniffing around a woman who, according to his very accurate business instincts, was trouble.

Dialing the number from memory, Cade sat back in his chair. Darius's house manager, Mrs. Tucker answered. "Andreas residence."

"Hey, baby. How's it going in the money capital of the world?"

Hey, baby? This was how he talked to staff?

Suzanne sniffed and tried to yank her skirt to a more proper place on her legs. Too late, she realized Cade would notice the action and that would only draw his gaze where she didn't want it.

She wanted to be taken seriously. Given a job. Yet this whole meeting had a weird feel to it, almost as if something had been going on that she'd missed.

"Can you get Darius for me?"

She pursed her lips. Straightened her spine.

Tried to look like a woman with something to offer a huge shipping conglomerate. She knew her "almost" art history degree hadn't given her a marketable skill, but she could type. She could organize. There were a million things she could do. Plus, she wasn't picky, or proud. She'd take what she could get.

Just then Cade's gaze met hers. Intense heat filled her. He was so good-looking that for a few seconds there, when they'd found themselves alone, before she'd told him about her shares of Andreas Holdings, she'd wondered what it would be like if they'd gone to find someplace to be alone for an entirely different reason than business....

She swallowed. Oh, good grief. Now she got it. In those few seconds, he'd been wondering, too. Or maybe planning.

That's why he'd locked the door!

Oh, no! He might have actually thought she'd brought him to his office to seduce him.

Well, too bad. She needed a job more than she needed a boyfriend—no, lover. He'd never be anybody's boyfriend, but she'd bet he'd happily be her lover.

Heat filled her. Her insides constricted then blossomed.

She had to stop thinking about that.

"Hey, Darius, it's me. I've got good news and bad news." A pause. "Well, the good news is I've found our mystery shareholder. The bad news is she wants a job. I'm going to put the phone on speaker." He hit a button on his phone then replaced the receiver.

"Darius, our shareholder is Suzanne Caldwell. She's across the desk from me."

"It's a pleasure to meet you, Ms. Caldwell."

Darius's voice was deep and smooth and had the tone of someone accustomed to being diplomatic. With Cade Andreas as a brother, he probably had to be.

"It's a pleasure to meet you, too, Mr. Andreas. I'm sorry to be trouble, but my grandmother died only a few months ago and the estate was a mess. She had spent more money than was coming in for the past several years—"

"Probably because Andreas Holdings stopped paying dividends."

"Maybe," Suzanne agreed. She sucked in a soft breath. "Anyway, I have a child. A baby girl, Mitzi, and I—we—"

"Of course, you need money. Perfectly understandable. You do understand, though, that Andreas Holdings isn't in a position to buy your shares."

Cade leaned back in his chair. Crossed his arms. Gave her one of those looks that could have melted butter.

Having realized where his mind had been when he locked the den door, Suzanne didn't get a shiver of fear from "that" look. Instead, her blood simmered.

She licked her lips. "I understand. I'm not approaching you to sell my shares."

Cade sat forward and leaned his arms on his desk. "She wants a job, Dar."

"As?"

Again Cade answered. "I know you can't drop her into a vice president position, but she's fairly smart."

Suzanne glanced up sharply. *He thought she was smart?*

"And," Cade continued, "I'm sure there are a lot of things she could do for us on an executive level. Something that would pay her enough to get a nice condo and a nanny for her baby."

Wow. He was being so kind. So considerate. So generous. Almost as if he liked her.

Her stomach filled with butterflies.

What if he liked her? What if this strong, sexy, smart man hadn't harassed her at the diner because he was the bossy overlord of the little piece of heaven he called Whiskey Springs, but because he'd been…interested…and his flirting skills were a little rusty?

She swallowed.

"There's got to be something she can do."

"Why don't you both fly up to New York City tomorrow morning so we can discuss it? You can be my guests at the house in Montauk Sunday night. Gino will be thrilled to see you, Cade. And Whitney loves company. Bring your daughter, Ms. Caldwell. It will be our pleasure."

With that Darius disconnected the call and silence reigned in Cade's office.

He leaned back in his chair. Rubbed his fingers across his forehead. Closed his eyes.

This wasn't at all what she'd had planned. And the thought that he might "like" her only added confusion to the mix. He was a gorgeous, sexy guy and she was attracted to him. But was she ready for anything to happen between them? After having been dumped only a little over a year ago?

No. She wasn't.

"I'm sorry."

"You didn't make the royal proclamation that we had to go to New York together. Darius did."

"I know, but your having to go to New York is my fault. I'd be happy to go by myself." She winced. "Except I don't have plane fare."

"I have an actual plane."

"Really?"

"Seven."

Her eyes widened. For a family that was broke, they certainly had more assets than she did.

"We'll leave at six. That should get us to the

house in Montauk before noon, considering we'll have to drive from the airstrip."

He rose from the desk. "Now, I have guests to attend to."

He walked out of the den without another word. Suzanne folded her hands on her lap not quite sure what she should do.

She was about to fly to New York City with a man who'd thought she'd brought him into his office to seduce him. A man who plainly had been willing to be seduced.

And he'd left before they could clear the air about their feelings.

Could she have botched this any worse?

CHAPTER FOUR

WHEN Suzanne's cell phone alarm woke her at four o'clock the next morning, she pulled the covers over her head. Explaining who she was to Cade had been a disaster. Now she had to fly to New York with him. That is, after she told Amanda Mae she couldn't work for the next few days—and might not be coming back to work at all.

Staying in bed sounded like a really good plan.

Unfortunately, Mitzi had heard the alarm, too, and her soft cries filled the room.

"I'm coming," she said, sliding out of bed. She fed the baby a bottle, dressed her in a happy yellow sundress with pink, blue and green ladybugs circling the hem, then took a shower and dressed herself in the blue suit she'd kept for interviews. Because, technically, she was going for an interview.

Ten minutes later, balancing a baby, a diaper bag, a suitcase packed with extra clothes for both her and Mitzi, and a car seat, she carefully walked down the outside stairway and into the diner.

Amanda Mae harrumphed. "What are you all dolled up for?"

She set the empty car seat on the floor. Walking to the cupboard where they now kept Mitzi's cereal, Suzanne avoided Amanda Mae's gaze. "I'm going to New York City with Cade Andreas."

She turned just in time to see Amanda Mae's big brown eyes pop and her mouth fall open. "What?"

"Oh, Amanda Mae. I am so sorry, but I have a confession to make."

"Look, honey, there isn't a woman in the world who could fault you for quitting a job as a waitress and running away with Cade Andreas. Even I'd let him put his boots under my bed and I haven't done the nasty in over a decade."

Thank God that made her laugh. "No. I'm not… He's not… We're…" She stopped. She had no idea what they were. He'd taken her part in the discussion with his brother. He'd made inroads with the company she couldn't have made for herself. And he was taking her to New York.

"Oh, come on. I told you I saw that spark between you. I think our boy Cade is sweet on you."

She swallowed, ignoring the heat that shimmered through her at the thought that Cade might actually feel something for her. Hadn't she thought the same thing herself the night before?

"We're going to New York to talk with his family. I own one-third of the company he and his half brothers inherited when their dad died."

Amanda Mae's eyes narrowed. "You're an heiress?"

Busying herself with preparing Mitzi's cereal, she said, "If you call someone who actually doesn't get any money from the estate they inherit an heiress, then, yes, I'm an heiress."

"You had an estate but didn't get any money?"

"My gram made some bad investments." She slid Mitzi into the swing and stooped down to begin spoon-feeding her. "Really bad. And she stopped getting dividends from the one company she thought she could always depend on." She didn't say from whom she stopped getting dividends to protect Cade and his brothers. "Three years went by with her losing money, but she never stopped her outrageous spending. So when she died I had to sell our home, our furniture, the art collections." She glanced down at her simple blue suit. "Even most of my clothes."

Crossing her arms on her chest, Amanda Mae said, "What does that have to do with going to New York?"

Scooping another spoonful of cereal into Mitzi's eager mouth, she cleared her throat. "I'm hoping that since I own one-third of their company, they'll give me a job."

Amanda Mae blew her breath out in disgust. "No matter how you slice it, you're leaving, and from what you're saying I don't even get any good gossip out of it."

"I'm not a hundred percent sure I'm leaving for good. They might not give me a job." She fed another bite to Mitzi as she continued in a rush. "So I may have to come back and continue working for you."

With a sad sigh, Amanda Mae turned away. "Yeah, well, I've still gotta call someone to come in to handle your shift this morning."

Suzanne's throat tightened. She liked Amanda Mae. There had been a click of something between them, an instant bond. It didn't feel right to be hoping to get another job. It felt even worse to have saddened her friend.

"I talked to your niece last night. She'll do the breakfast crowd."

The diner door opened and Suzanne's gaze swung over as Cade walked in. He wore his usual jeans and T-shirt. But today, remembering Amanda Mae's comment that he was sweet on her, the little zing of attraction she always felt for him morphed into a breath-stealing whoosh. He could have any woman on the face of the earth. If he was interested in her, it was equal parts of flattering and confusing. She really wasn't ready for another relationship. But how did anybody turn down a man like Cade Andreas?

Amanda Mae glanced sideways and saw him, too. Still, she didn't turn around and face Suzanne. Her voice was gruff when she said,

"Okay. Thanks for taking care of that. You scoot now."

Suzanne's heart turned over in her chest. Even with Cade waiting for her in the dining room, she couldn't get her feet to move. Still she had to follow through with her stocks. If owning one-third interest gave her enough clout to get her a good job she owed it to Mitzi to take it.

She scooped Mitzi out of the swing. "I'll stop in when we get back." She smiled ruefully. "To let you know if I'm still your waitress."

Amanda Mae didn't turn around. "Sure."

With that, Suzanne walked into the dining room.

Cade didn't say a word, simply motioned for Suzanne to follow him outside. At the door, he took the car seat and diaper bag from her and she carried Mitzi.

He opened the back door of his extended cab truck and slid the car seat inside. "I know this thing gets buckled in but I don't know how to do it." He held out his hands. "So give me the baby while you install it."

She slid Mitzi to him, careful to keep from accidentally brushing hands, and efficiently installed the car seat. When she turned to take Mitzi from him she noticed he was studying her. "Haven't you ever seen a baby before?"

He smiled ruefully and handed Mitzi to her. "Yes and no. Yes, I've seen a baby. But it's been a while." He paused, then added, "She's cute."

If that was a peace offering for leaving her in his office the night before, or a way for them to get back to a natural footing with each other, it worked. "Thanks. I like her."

He chuckled. "No kidding."

Once Mitzi was buckled in, he ushered her up to the passenger seat then rounded the hood and climbed in himself.

Emotionally confused after her talk with Amanda Mae and not wanting to break the fragile peace between herself and Cade, Suzanne stayed quiet. But the silence in the truck became oppressive, nudging her to say something—anything—to break it. Blessedly, his phone rang.

Wearing an earpiece, he didn't have to pick up. He said simply, "Hey, Eric, isn't it a little early for you and monster dog?"

As he spoke, her gaze strayed over to him. It wasn't often that he was occupied and she grabbed the opportunity to study him without worry. She took in the stretch of the denim across his strong thighs. The way his T-shirt hugged the well-defined muscles of his chest. His easy competence driving.

What would it be like to be dating this man?

Her breath stalled in her chest. The blood in her veins crackled to life. He was, without a doubt one of the sexiest men she'd ever seen. But date him?

Okay. It would probably be fun, since she guessed he'd never be boring. But she didn't know him. And she didn't even really know that he liked her. All she had were suspicions based on Amanda Mae's observation and the guess she'd made the night before that he thought she'd brought him back to his office to seduce him. That was trouble enough. She had to stop thinking there was more to it.

When they arrived at a private airstrip, she jumped out of the truck and immediately grabbed Mitzi and headed for the plane. Though she'd

flown in private planes before, Cade's was one
step beyond what she was accustomed to. Five
butterscotch leather seats were arranged throughout the cabin. Two sat across from a shiny yel-
lowish wood entertainment unit with a big-screen
TV. Two sat by a bar made of the same shiny
wood. One in the back was connected to a desk.

Cade strode to the one in the back and tossed
a black leather briefcase on the desk.

Ten seconds later, the pilot jogged up the steps,
followed by a female copilot.

"I'm Dave. This is Jenny." The pretty red-
haired copilot nodded. "The weather looks good.
We should be in New York in a few hours." He
smiled at Suzanne. "Buckle yourselves in."

With that he and Jenny entered the cockpit.
Cade pulled two files out of his briefcase, opened
them and never looked up again.

She suppressed a sigh. She understood he was
ignoring her. She supposed that could actually
work to their advantage. If they were both on
their best behavior, they wouldn't risk another
misunderstanding. But, sheesh, it was going to
be a long, boring ride if they didn't talk.

Hours later, Suzanne almost cheered when they landed. From the plane's window, she could see a man in tan pants and a white dress shirt standing by a long black limo, holding a toddler. A woman in capris and a frilly blouse stood beside them. All three wore sunglasses. The toddler squirmed.

The captain and cocaptain said goodbye as Cade walked down the three steps to the tarmac, then took the big diaper bag from Suzanne and caught her hand to help her down the steps. When his fingers closed around hers, their eyes met. The hot June breeze drifted around her. Warmth radiated from their joined hands.

Okay. He might be ignoring her but they were still attracted to each other and last night they'd both jumped to some bad conclusions. She had to do something about the awkwardness between them. And quickly before they weren't alone anymore.

"Look, I'm sorry I gave you the wrong impression last night."

Dropping her hand, he turned to walk to the limo. "What wrong impression? You own one-third of my family's company. No way I could get the wrong impression about a fact."

"So you're not mad about the other?"

He stopped and faced her, his expression shuttered. "What 'other'?"

Ah, so he wasn't ignoring her. He was pretending the beginning part of their conversation, the click of the lock on the den door, the hot look in his eyes never happened?

Actually, that would be one way for them to get beyond the awkwardness.

"I was just pleased you took my part with your brother last night."

He huffed out a breath, propped his hands on his hips and looked up at the blue sky. "It was the right thing to do. The fair thing."

Her pulse stilled. Her battered ego fluttered to life. Fairness might be commonplace for him, but she couldn't remember the last time anyone had truly treated her fairly. Except Amanda Mae. Still, there was no way to explain that to him without getting maudlin or too personal. And after her last attempt at a personal conversation with this guy—well, she knew better.

So she simply said, "Thanks. I appreciated it."

As they approached the limo, the man Suzanne assumed was Darius stepped forward. He took the diaper bag from Cade. "Nice to see you, brother." He turned to Suzanne. "And this must be Suzanne and Mitzi."

From his welcoming smile, it was easy for Suzanne to see Darius was a nice guy. With black hair and dark eyes similar to Cade's, he definitely had a family resemblance to his half brother. "Yes. I'm Suzanne Caldwell. It's nice to meet you."

"This is Whitney, my wife, and our son, Gino."

Whitney grinned and pointed at Mitzi. "Can I hold her?"

Suzanne laughed. "Yes. She gets a little heavy after hours and hours on a plane."

After a quick scowl at Cade, as if chastising him for not helping with the baby, Whitney took Mitzi. "Well, hello there, Miss Mitzi."

Mitzi immediately began to cry.

"I'll take her back."

Whitney returned the baby to Suzanne. "She'll

get used to me, but now's not the time to force the issue."

"Cook has made lunch," Darius said, motioning for everyone to enter the limo when the driver opened the door.

When they were settled, they took off toward Darius and Whitney's home. Suzanne spent most of her time entertaining Mitzi, while Darius, Whitney and Cade made small talk.

Out of the corner of her eye, she studied their interaction. A brother and his wife, teasing another brother who gave as good as he got. He wasn't rude, the way he'd been the day she'd met him. He wasn't overbearing, as he'd been the day he'd come into the diner. He was nice.

Normal.

Huh! She almost snorted a laugh. Normal? He owned a ranch, a town and seven planes. And a big chunk of a shipping conglomerate. He might wear boots and jeans, but he was savvy, sharp. Sophisticated.

A sizzle of excitement sparked through her. She wasn't just attracted by his looks. She liked that he was smart. She liked that he was savvy.

She almost groaned. Being around him must be making her brain soft because it didn't matter if she liked him or not. She'd been burned by the last man she'd been involved with and now had a baby to raise. She needed a job. Those were the things she should be thinking about. Not how attractive he was. Or even how smart.

The "house" in Montauk was actually an oceanside estate. They stepped out of the limo to the sounds of waves crashing on the shore. Whitney showed Suzanne to the suite of rooms she would be using during her stay and then escorted her and Mitzi to the dining room where Gino ate macaroni and cheese and the four adults ate spinach salads with crusty homemade bread.

After lunch, Whitney suggested they leave Gino and Mitzi with the nanny for an afternoon nap, while she and Suzanne took a stroll on the beach.

Darius led Cade to the office, and he plopped down on a seat in front of Darius's desk. "Okay. So you've met her. What are we going to do?"

Before the question was fully out of his mouth, the office door opened and Nick, the other

Andreas half brother, walked in. "Mrs. Tucker
sent Michael to the nursery and Maggie to the
beach where Whitney and Suzanne are walking," he said, referring to his fiancée and her
nine-month-old son. "She told me the men were
meeting in the office."

Darius gestured to the empty chair in front of
his desk. "Take a seat. We're talking about shareholder number five."

Wearing cutoff jeans and flip-flops, Nick
plopped down on the seat beside Cade. "Ah, the
mysterious Suzanne Caldwell, the one who technically owns the most stock."

"Individually." Cade snarled. "Together we still
own two-thirds."

Nick laughed and addressed Darius. "Touchy."

"Did you see Ms. Caldwell?"

Nick shook his head. Darius laughed. "Just
wait. One look and you'll know why our brother
is behaving like a bear with a thorn in his paw."

"I'm not behaving like a bear." Cade popped
out of his seat and began to pace. "I'm just
concerned. She tried to sell her stock. Nobody
wanted it, but once our annual statement comes

out and everybody sees profits are up, she'll get offers. And Andreas Holdings isn't in a position to be one of them."

"Cool your jets, Cade. Nick and I decided we shouldn't wait for the company to have enough money to purchase the stock. We should buy it as individuals." Darius leaned back in his chair. "We know you could have your share of the money tomorrow. Unfortunately, Nick and I aren't that lucky. It will take us some time to get that kind of cash together."

Cade turned. "How much time?"

"I think eighteen months. After you called last night, I called Nick and we ran some numbers and we both think we can have our portions in eighteen months."

Cade groaned. "That's not good enough. She's broke. Seriously broke."

"That's why we've come up with some other ideas. First, I think you should take a look at her finances. Maybe she has assets she doesn't know about?"

He shook his head. "From what she told me accountants and attorneys pretty much pillaged every asset in her grandmother's estate to pay debts. I don't think I'm going to find anything they didn't."

Nick shrugged. "Look anyway. You never know. Her grandmother might have put some things in Suzanne's name alone. Things that might not have turned up on a search of her grandmother's assets."

Darius picked up a pencil and tapped it against his desk blotter. "Second, because we won't be solvent enough to buy her out for at least another year, we're going to have to strike a deal to buy her shares eighteen months from now when we have the cash."

"What kind of deal?"

"We'd set the purchase price of her stock at its value the day her grandmother died. We'll offer a million dollars as a holding fee. Then in eighteen months we'll pay the balance."

Relieved, Cade nodded, but Darius continued. "The job of persuading her to take the deal falls to you, Cade. Nick and I are running the company. We never pushed you to do any more than what you could squeeze in. So it's your turn to step up."

Nick grinned. "Suzanne Caldwell is all yours."

"And you talk to her today," Darius said. "As soon as you get a private minute with her, so she can stop worrying and enjoy her time here."

Suzanne, Whitney and Maggie returned from their walk on the beach chatting like three long-lost friends. Whitney had explained that Gino was actually Darius, Nick and Cade's half brother and that their father had been killed in an accident with Gino's mother. So Whitney and Darius had adopted him.

Maggie had explained that she had been married to Nick at eighteen. She'd left him when the brothers' absentee father, Stephone Andreas, had offered him five million dollars to divorce her, and now they were back together, planning a wedding in four weeks.

Suddenly Suzanne's story of having been taken advantage of by a sleazy university professor didn't sound all that crazy. And when Maggie and Whitney gasped in horror then sympathized,

Suzanne actually felt wanted. Normal. Just like one of the girls.

They entered the nursery talking about how much alike Darius, Nick and Cade were even though they were entirely different. Darius had grown up working for Andreas Holdings and had stayed on as CEO and Chairman of the Board after their father died. Nick owned a manufacturing plant in North Carolina. And Cade was a billionaire. He'd taken the five million dollars their dad offered and he'd made himself a very wealthy man. Knowing he didn't depend on Andreas Holdings for cash explained a lot about his life in Whiskey Springs.

Both women also admitted it had been Cade who'd more or less nudged Nick and Darius into seeing the truth about their relationships. Which struck Suzanne as interesting. For a guy who wasn't married himself, he certainly seemed to have a high opinion of marriage.

By dinnertime, she was totally comfortable—until she saw the seating arrangement, which put her beside Cade. She knew his family wasn't matchmaking. Darius sat at the head of the table with Gino's high chair at his right. Whitney sat across from him, at the other end of the table. Nick, Maggie and Michael took up the entire left side. With Mitzi in the nursery with the nanny, she and Cade were the only two people left and there were only two chairs remaining. Both on the right side. It was simple math, not matchmaking.

Cade politely pulled out her chair. She accepted with a smile.

But after only five minutes of sitting beside him, a little hum of attraction set up housekeeping in her bloodstream, if only because of proximity. He was so close she could touch him if she wanted. So close he could touch her.

She told herself it was ridiculous to be plotting an accidental elbow brush. Told herself to stop being attracted to a guy she shouldn't want. But the truth was, after hearing Whitney and Maggie talking about Cade that afternoon, she didn't believe he was half the narcissist she'd originally thought. And what was the deal with him encouraging his brothers to marry Whitney and Maggie? She'd thought for a sure a rich, handsome guy like Cade would push a playboy lifestyle. Not just for himself but for his brothers, so he'd have guys to go to Vegas with. The fact that he hadn't made him seem like a whole different person to her.

A likable person.

A person very different from the professor who had dumped her.

And maybe she shouldn't be as afraid of this attraction as she thought.

The dinner of honey-lemon rack of lamb and red potatoes, served with good wine and mocha cream pie for dessert, was delicious and the conversation pleasant. Nick was a charming Southern gentleman who loved horses and enjoyed a good story. Darius was a businessman to the core, but Whitney easily mellowed him out, got him to laugh and talk about things other than employee disputes and prospective customers.

But the entire time Suzanne was aware of Cade. His size. His sexy Southern drawl. The times he joined in the conversation. The times he didn't.

She'd never felt as curious about a man before. She knew the attraction was to blame. Still, no matter how many times she told herself to stop wondering about him, she couldn't.

When dinner was through, Darius tapped his knife to his wineglass and said, "I'd like to propose a toast, but you'll notice my wife isn't having wine tonight."

Suzanne blinked. She glanced at Whitney, who had pinkened endearingly and the realization hit her the same time that it hit Maggie. Both gasped and simultaneously said, "You're pregnant!"

Whitney clapped with glee. "Yes! I'd wanted to tell you this afternoon but Darius and I had decided to make the announcement to everyone at once."

From there pandemonium broke out. Nick congratulated Darius and kissed Whitney. Maggie and Suzanne continued talking simultaneously. Cade held back, but only for a second. *He'd* wanted a baby. He'd wanted a black-haired, blue-eyed little boy. Or a blond-haired, brown-eyed little girl. They'd never figured out if it was he or Ashley who couldn't conceive because they'd found her cancer as soon as her testing began. Not wanting to upset her, he hadn't even gone for tests. So he didn't even know if he could have kids.

Now Nick had a son and would have more children. Maggie was an earth-mother. She'd happily tend to six kids. Go to soccer games. Be a den mother for Boy Scouts.

Darius had Gino…plus a new baby on the way.

And Cade would probably never have kids. No sons. No daughters. He was the one who hadn't pretended to be a big, bad playboy, as his two older brothers had. He was the one who had married his high school sweetheart, tried to start a family, longed to be the dad Stephone Andreas never was to him. He'd had visions of coaching Little League, visions of watching his daughter dance in recitals, visions of rocking babies in the rocking chair his mom had kept in her bedroom until he'd built his big house. Then she'd given it to him as a housewarming gift. Only to have it sit empty in an unused nursery.

Still, he swallowed back the injustice of it all and rose. He walked over to Darius, slapped him on the back and said all the right things.

When the commotion died down, Darius and

Whitney excused themselves to get Gino ready for bed, and Nick and Maggie drifted away. Cade knew exactly what they were doing. He'd been ordered to take Suzanne under his wing and tell her the brothers' plan.

Talking to her was the last thing he wanted to do. Were the choice his, he'd grab one of Darius's best bottles of whiskey, amble down to the beach and get himself drunk enough that he wouldn't care that all his plans for a family had been snatched away from him.

Instead, he had to handle Andreas brothers' business.

Knowing that Mitzi was in the nursery with the nanny, he turned to Suzanne. "How about a walk on the beach?"

She faced him with a surprised look.

Because that sounded a little too much like a romantic overture, he cleared up any misunderstanding. "My brothers want me to tell you what we've decided about your stock."

"Oh." Her eyes clouded with something he couldn't quite identify. Disappointment, maybe? "Okay."

Pretending not to notice the expression in her eyes, he led her out the French doors, past the shimmering pool and down the path to the shore.

"I'm so happy for Darius and Whitney," she said, facing Cade with a grin. "They're wonderful parents to Gino."

He sucked in a breath. The lonely, empty feeling of loss returned, but he shut that down and forced himself to be happy for his brother. "Yes. They're great parents."

"And little Michael. What a scamp! He crawls everywhere." She peeked over at him again. "I can understand why Nick and Maggie decided to wait a few months to get married." She kicked the sand with the toe of her sandal. "Not only is he big enough now to stay with Nick's mom while they honeymoon, but they really wanted a summer wedding. On the beach." She glanced at him again. "Nick lives at the beach, too. In North Carolina. They grew up together at the beach, you know?"

He and Ashley had grown up together, too, so, yes, he knew. He knew all about first loves and how wonderful they could be. But for once he wasn't thinking about Ashley. He was thinking about Suzanne. He'd never heard that lilt in her voice before. She'd obviously had a good time with Maggie and Whitney. And even as he wanted to wallow in misery, he felt an odd stirring in his chest. Almost as if he'd been hoping for her to be happy and now that she was it made him happy. Proud. As if he'd had some part in it.

He scowled. He did not want her happiness to matter to him. It was bad enough he was in charge of her welfare. He didn't want to be manager of her happiness, too. He might have been forced to help her, but he refused to get involved with her. She was a pretty, sexy thorn in his side. A temptation he didn't want nor need.

"Are you going to stop talking long enough for me to tell you what my brothers decided this afternoon?"

She stepped back as if he'd slapped her. "I was just making conversation."

Okay, now he'd hurt her. He hadn't meant to. He'd just wanted this over with.

He stopped, ran his hand along the back of his

neck. "Some of this you're going to like. Some of it you might hate."

"Just say it."

The hurt that wobbled through her voice hit him right in the heart and froze it. He hated to see women hurt or, worse, cry.

He sighed. "Look, I'm sorry. I know I'm gruff sometimes. It's just the way I am. But the bottom line is we want to buy back your stock. We can't afford it now, but we're willing to give you a holding fee."

Her eyes widened, lit with joy, and his heart began to beat again.

"You're going to give me a holding fee?"

"Yes, a million dollars."

Her mouth fell open. "A million dollars!"

"The company is improving. Once our annual statement comes out, you'll have real suitors who will be after your stock. Which is why we intend to be able to buy you out in eighteen months."

"Eighteen months!"

"We'll pay you the prevailing price on your grandmother's date of death."

She pressed her hand to her chest. "Oh, my gosh!"

"So you won't have to worry about the holding fee. Though it will be deducted from the amount you get for the stock, it'll be a drop in the bucket compared to the hundred million dollars or so you'll get in the sale."

Her face lit with so much joy that he relaxed.

"A hundred million dollars! I can get a house! A new car. Not worry about—"

But suddenly the joy faded, her eyes narrowed and she frowned. "Wait."

"What?"

"Does this mean I don't get a job?"

"This means you don't need a job."

"The hell, I don't! You're telling me you 'believe' you'll be able to buy my stock in eighteen months, but you don't know. All the agreements in the world mean nothing if you can't get the money together when you think you will. *Nothing* in life is certain."

He couldn't argue that.

"So you can't tell me for sure you'll be buying the stock. Your holding fee is more of a hope that you'll be able to buy the stock in eighteen months."

"Why don't we cross that bridge when we come to it? A million dollars is a lot of money—"

"Yes. And I appreciate it. But I watched my grandmother lose *hundreds* of millions of dollars in a few short years when the stock market began to crumble and Andreas Holdings quit paying dividends." She sighed. "I don't trust easy money. I'd like a job. Then I'd have the security of earning a steady salary, no matter how long it takes you to pull together the cash for my shares."

"Yeah, well, you don't have a marketable skill."

"I can type! I can research. I could even be a receptionist. I'm not picky—"

Something inside of Cade snapped. As he watched her pretty mouth telling him things that didn't actually seem unreasonable—but had to be unreasonable because they were not the plan he and his brothers had worked out—his frustration combined with the futility of arguing with this woman, who was too darned pretty for his own good, and he totally lost his hold on common sense.

All he wanted was for her to stop talking, and the quickest route to that, his hormones assured him, was to kiss her. Before he really thought the plan through, his arm snaked around her waist and hauled her to him as his head descended until his mouth met her soft, sweet lips.

Every muscle in his body tensed. He'd intended to surprise her into silence, instead *his* breathing stuttered, *his* chest tightened, *his* gut squeezed. Her soft lips drew him in, causing him to forget his mission. Especially when her lips seemed to invite him to taste more, take more.

Temptation and desire met and merged. She wasn't stopping him. And she tasted so good. So perfect—

Perfect?

For what?

She was a single mom. A business associate now. A woman he couldn't love then leave.

He knew better than to kiss her.

He *knew* better!

He jerked away, breaking the kiss, and stepped back. Shocked by his behavior, he ran his hand along the back of his neck. Suzanne stared up at him with wide eyes and lips dewy from his kiss.

"Okay, look. I'm sorry. That shouldn't have happened."

She simply continued to stare at him. And he knew he'd given her the wrong idea. Romantic ideas. Damn. Why did he always behave like an idiot around her?

He took another step back, away from her. "Here's the deal. I was married."

She blinked, as if absorbing that, then said, "And she hurt you, right?"

"No. She died." He said it gruffly, angrily. He'd learned long ago that anger was the best way to keep the other, more dangerous emotions at bay. "But even before she got sick, I proved to both of us that I wasn't any great shakes as a husband. She was the love of my life and I treated her shabbily."

He sucked in a breath, wished she'd stop looking at him with big blue eyes that had gone from sharp with desire to soft with sadness. For him. God, he hated pity.

"Get any romantic ideas you might have out

of your head because I'm not in the market for a relationship and you shouldn't want me."

When she only blinked, Cade knew he wasn't getting through, so he pushed harder. "Okay, let me tell you a few things that never made it to the diner gossip because they're things I don't tell anyone." He held up his index finger. "Number one, I spent the first two years of my marriage traveling to build my fortune."

His second finger snapped up. "Number two, you'd have thought that after she got sick I would have settled in, settled down, but no. I wanted Beacher's Oil so bad that I pursued it like the Holy Grail and one night while I was sweet-talking my way into a deal, she faded away. She was gone when I got back."

When he stopped, the salty air rang with the sound of the waves. He scrubbed his hand down his face, surprised he'd admitted so much, but knowing he'd had to to make it abundantly clear to her why she shouldn't feel sorry for him. Shouldn't feel *anything* for him.

"Cade, I'm so sorry."

At her soft apology, he realized that even his

expanded explanation hadn't worked because now her big blue eyes were rimmed with tears.

"Forget it. Just understand I was no good as a husband and stay the hell away from me."

CHAPTER FIVE

HE TURNED and began striding up the beach. Suzanne watched him bound away, an achy pain squeezing her heart. He hadn't fooled her with the gruff voice and the straightforward proclamations. She could see from the tortured look on his face that his wife's death had been brutal on him. It was no wonder he behaved oddly around her. He was attracted to her and didn't want to be.

He stopped, faced her. His dark hair blew in the breeze off the ocean. His dark eyes bored into her. "Are you coming? I'm not going to stand here all night. If you want to walk up by yourself that's fine. But it's dark and I don't generally leave women alone in the dark."

She scrambled across the shifting sand to catch up with him, confusion warring with the sympathy she felt for him. Losing her grandmother had changed her life, filled her with grief, filled her with *anger*. She couldn't even imagine how hard it would be to lose a spouse.

At the French doors off the patio into the den, Cade paused, waiting for her to get to the door before he opened it for her.

They stepped into the dimly lit den only to discover Nick and Maggie sat on the brown leather sofa, Whitney sat on a wing chair and Darius was behind the bar.

"Drink?"

Suzanne's gaze swung back to Cade, as if looking for his preference, but he walked away without a glance in her direction.

"I'll have a beer and I'll get it myself."

Carrying two beers and a glass of wine, Darius walked to the conversation group. He handed the wine to Maggie and one of the beers to Nick then sat on the chair beside Whitney's. "Great. I love it when someone wants to play bartender. Suzanne, just give your request to Cade."

"I'm fine. Thanks." Not exactly sure what to do, she hovered near the door.

Whitney waved her over, motioning to the empty love seat. "Please. Sit."

Suzanne glanced at the love seat then back at Cade. The only seat left in the room would smash them against each other.

It didn't matter. He'd made himself perfectly clear. He wasn't interested. He'd had the love of his life. He'd been a bad husband. And after her ordeal with Mitzi's dad, she was also smart enough not to want to get involved with a guy who boldly admitted he wasn't husband material…

Except that kiss had been amazing. Her breathing had stopped and all her senses had intensified. He'd drawn her in, clouded her brain, liquefied her limbs with one soft press of his mouth to hers.

They weren't just attracted. They were smokin' hot attracted.

But they were also smart. Too smart to get involved. He was a bad bet as a romantic partner. With her life in total chaos, she wasn't exactly looking for a romance, let alone a guy who might be attracted to her but didn't want to be. They had more than enough motivation to stay away from each other, even squished together on a couch.

She ambled to the love seat. Cade slid from behind the bar with his opened bottle of beer. But he didn't come over to sit with her. He headed for the cold fireplace.

Really? He was going to be that petty?

But a little voice inside her head cautioned her not to be so sure he was being petty. That kiss had knocked her socks off. Surely it must have had the same effect on him.

What if he didn't trust himself to control himself?

What if *that* was really why he was angry?

"So, I'm guessing Cade told you about our plans for you."

Something about the authoritative tone of Darius's voice raised her hackles, but she told herself not to be so sensitive. Even though the Andreas brothers hadn't offered a job, their suggested holding fee had been generous and she needed to think it through. Though she'd popped off with Cade, she couldn't simply turn down a million dollars because it wasn't what she'd expected.

"I thought your offer was very generous, but—"

"But she's a bit miffed that we didn't pony up a job."

When Cade interrupted her, Suzanne could have sighed. His interpretation of her reaction might have been correct, but now that things were sinking in, she wasn't quite so adamant. Besides, she could speak for herself.

"I don't think *miffed* is the right word. *Cautious* is better. I never expected to be offered a holding fee and I need—"

"You were like a bull snorting fire out on the beach. You're not happy with our offer."

Suzanne scorched him with a look. She might not have been happy with the offer, but that was her gut reaction. Not a real decision. Plus, his way of shutting her up had been to kiss her.

How would he like her telling his brothers that?

Darius quietly broke into her stare down with Cade. "What concerns you?"

"I asked for a job because I want some security. What happens in eighteen months if the company doesn't rebound the way you think it should?"

"It will," Nick put in, as calm and serious as

Darius. "But that doesn't matter. The company itself isn't buying your shares. We're buying them from our personal accounts. And we'll easily have the money in eighteen months."

"And once you get that money, you're back to being a very wealthy woman," Darius reminded her. "If we employ you, you'll need to move to New York. You'll have to get a condo and a nanny. And just when you have yourself settled, we'll have pulled the money together to buy you out and you'll have to fire your nanny and sell your condo when you move back to Atlanta. If you take the holding fee, you can simply go back now, reenroll in school."

He had a point. With a million dollars she could go back to school....

She frowned. The thought of returning to the same university where Bill Baker taught was not a pleasant one. But her old school wasn't the only university in the country. With a million dollars she could enroll just about anywhere.

She could finish her degree and then take a year of more practical classes. Like accounting. Or maybe business management. This rough patch in her life had proven she needed to be employable. If nothing else, somehow or another at the end of these eighteen months she intended to have a job.

Nick smiled. "We won't let you down."

"Plus, you might just discover you're not as broke as you think," Darius added. "You could find assets you didn't know about when Cade takes a look at the big picture of your finances."

Her eyes narrowed. "Cade's taking a look at my finances?"

Darius smiled. "Your grandmother could have opened accounts for you that she forgot. Accounts that wouldn't show up when her estate ran a check because they'd have your name and social security number on them, not hers. So I've assigned Cade to look into that."

Just when things started to fall into place in her head, she somehow ended up connected to Cade again. She shifted on the love seat. "I don't want Cade poking into my finances."

Cade snorted as if the idea didn't please him, either.

Whitney shook her head, rose and sat beside

Suzanne. "I'm going to apologize for my husband and his brothers." She caught both of her hands. "I know Darius has a tendency to bulldoze situations and I'm guessing Cade didn't explain this well." She glared at Cade.

He shrugged. "I actually never got a chance to make much of an explanation."

"The way Darius explained this to me," Whitney said, "Cade himself wouldn't be looking at your books. He's got a staff of accountants who would be examining the records, searching for lost accounts, that kind of thing."

"Maybe I should hire some accountants myself."

Cade huffed out a laugh. "Why waste money on accountants when I have them at my disposal?"

She licked her lips. That was true. She might be getting a lot of money eventually. But right now she was getting only a portion of that money and she couldn't be reckless. If she was careful now, in a few short months she and Mitzi would be financially secure.

"Okay."

Whitney's eyebrows rose. "Okay?"

"I'll take the money. I'll take the help of Cade's accountants. I'll spend the next semester finishing my degree and the year after that I'll take classes that might lead me to a real job."

From across the room Cade said, "You won't need it."

But she ignored him. Just as he'd said, he wasn't right for her. *They* weren't right for each other. Sure, they were sexually attracted, but she absolutely, positively did not want to be involved with him. She understood he was sad and angry about his wife's death, but why he thought he could take that out on her was a total mystery. If she ever got romantically involved again, it would be with someone who would really love her and appreciate her.

And Cade Andreas did not fit that bill.

A few minutes after midnight, Cade was running chalk along the tip of his pool stick when Whitney and Maggie pleaded tiredness. Suzanne had long ago gone upstairs to check on Mitzi and simply hadn't returned. But now Darius and Nick also said their good-nights and strolled off to bed with Whitney and Maggie.

Perfectly happy to have a few minutes by himself, Cade decided to have one last beer before he went to his suite upstairs. Unfortunately, he only got halfway through before Nick returned.

"I thought you were all snuggled up with the future Mrs. for the night."

"She's showering." Nick ambled into the room and fell to the seat on the sofa beside Cade. "I think you and I need one of those little talks like the one we had when you told me I had to pick up my end of the slack for Andreas Holdings."

"Not hardly, bud. You and Darius already had your little talk with me about helping Suzanne for the good of Andreas Holdings, and you see how well that went over."

Nick went on as if he hadn't spoken. "Tonight when Darius and I were trying to persuade her to take our money, we dangled going back to school in front of her."

Cade shrugged. "It worked a hell of a sight better than the talk I had with her." He vividly remembered how that ended. With a kiss. His intention had been to get her to stop talking and all he'd done was awaken his own damned hormones. "Our offer might have surprised her at first, but now she seems happy to take it."

"Yeah," Nick said, drawing out the one syllable into a long, skeptical word. "The problem is Maggie has some concerns about Suzanne going back to Atlanta."

"Maggie has some concerns?"

"Apparently they had some long talks today. From the things Suzanne said, Maggie believes Suzanne returning to her old school isn't a good idea. Mitzi's father is a professor there and apparently he made her life miserable enough that she had to quit. The guy's a snake and Maggie thinks it wouldn't be good for Suzanne to even see him."

"And you want me to...what?" For the love of God, had Nick not already noticed that he was *not* the person to talk to Suzanne?

"Pour on some of your rich Texan charm and persuade her to stay at your ranch with you. There has to be a university near Whiskey Springs that she can attend, somewhere she can transfer her credits."

He gaped at his brother. Now he knew Nick was insane…

Except Nick hadn't actually seen the discussion he'd had with Suzanne. He hadn't seen how Suzanne had gotten her back up. He hadn't seen Cade lose his head and kiss her.

And it would be a cold day in hell before Cade told him.

He snorted a laugh. "Right. We've already nudged her into thinking about going home. It's too late to change her mind. She wants to return to Atlanta."

"Maybe not. Just because that's where her school was, it doesn't mean she wants to go to Atlanta. She might have simply been happy at the thought of having a plan and somewhere to go."

"There are lots of good schools. In other cities."

"She has no family, Cade. Even if she stays away from the creep who fathered her baby and moves to another city, she's still got a boatload of problems. Who's going to watch Mitzi? Who's going to answer baby questions? At the very least, your staff could babysit while she attends classes." He shook his head. "It just doesn't feel right to send her off into the world alone. Not when she's one of us."

"One of us?"

"As long as she owns Andreas stock, she's one of us."

Cade sucked in a breath. If there was one thing their father's death had instilled in them, it was loyalty. With that reminder, he felt a brush of guilt. But just a brush because there was one very good reason Nick and Maggie's plan wouldn't work. "And how am I supposed to persuade her to transfer to a university near Whiskey Springs and stay with me? We might see her as 'one of us' but she barely knows us."

"You could tell her you need her close in case your accountants have questions."

The collar of Cade's shirt suddenly got too tight. That idea might actually work.

"She's one of us, Cade." Nick rose. "And Maggie believes she's lost. Alone. We want her to be comfortable. Not to be struggling through her last year of school with no one to help her with her baby, when you've got a whole town at your disposal."

He left the room and Cade flopped back on the sofa. He could picture having Suzanne living in his home. He'd vacillate between behaving like an angry bear and a hungry panther, slithering through his house, following her scent, itching to touch her. Hadn't that kiss on the beach proven he couldn't control himself around her?

Damn straight it had.

He was not—absolutely was not—inviting her to live with him.

Except...

What if she was alone? What if she really would be struggling to go to classes and care for her baby? What if she had no one to talk to? No one to call if Mitzi got sick. No one to even ask questions about raising her baby.

He told himself to stop obsessing. Suzanne was a smart, independent woman who would be fine. She *wanted* to be on her own. Hadn't she said as much at least three times?

* * *

Monday afternoon, after a round of goodbyes at the limo Darius had sent to take them to the airport, Suzanne and Cade made the ride to the airstrip in total silence. When they boarded the plane, Cade again sat at the desk in the rear, his head down, his focus on the papers in three open files.

Closing her eyes, Suzanne made herself comfortable on her seat. But after they were in the air, Cade's voice drifted over to her.

"I know this weekend didn't turn out the way you'd hoped. But my brothers are genuinely trying to help you. They're nice guys. Even if you don't like me, there's no reason to be suspicious of them."

She glanced at Mitzi, who slept in her carrier, then back at Cade. She hadn't been able to sleep the night before. Not just because she'd agreed to take a million dollars to hold her stock and now had a direction for her life. But because she'd begun to remember some of the things Whitney and Maggie had told her about Cade. Things that had caused her to see him in a different light.

Like how he'd helped his two brothers see they

were crazy about Whitney and Maggie and it was time to settle down. After her little tiff with Cade on the beach, she now knew he'd done that because he'd been married and understood a little more about life and love than his older brothers. But that didn't diminish the fact that he'd come to Whitney's and Maggie's aid. Just as he'd come to her aid the night she'd told him she was the missing shareholder, explaining to Darius that she needed a job.

He loved Gino. He loved little Michael. He teased and bantered with his brothers and their wives, but in a fun, brotherly sort of way.

If it hadn't been for that little tiff on the beach and the way he'd treated her after, she'd probably like him right now. And not just as a friend, but... well, romantically.

"I'm not suspicious of your brothers."

"Really?"

She shook her head and laughed softly. "Why would you think that when I took their offer?"

"Because you're quiet."

She pointed at the open files on his desk. "Yeah, well, you have work to do."

"And I've got plenty of time to get to it. Right now, I just want to make sure you're clear about our offer. That you don't have questions. That you're okay with everything."

Before this weekend she might have thought he was goading her, or thought she was too dumb to understand a simple deal. Today she knew he wasn't like that. If he was asking, it was out of genuine concern. Her heart got a little tug, but she ignored it. He'd made himself perfectly clear. He wasn't interested. And she had too many things on her plate right now to regret his choice.

"I understand everything your brothers told me this weekend."

"Good."

"Good…" She paused. Actually, she might understand everything about their deal, but there was one little bitty thing she didn't get about the Andreas brothers themselves. It was none of her business, but the truth was, with all the nice things Cade did for his brothers, his one omission seemed odd, out of character.

"Actually I have thought of something I might need to have cleared up."

"Like what?"

Marshaling her courage, she said, "Like you probably have five times the money your brothers have—"

"More like ten."

"So why don't you just buy me out? If you're all so worried about my stock getting into the wrong hands, why not just buy my stock and be done with me?"

He didn't even hesitate. "Because you own one-third of the company. My brothers and I each own one-sixth. If I buy you out and add my one-sixth to your one-third, I own half the company. We'd no longer be equals. I won't do that to them."

She blinked. Wow. If she had any questions about how he felt about his brothers they'd all just been answered. Their bond meant more to him than the possibility of losing her stock. Their connection meant more to him than money.

Maybe his wife's death had taught him a lesson?

Silence reigned again. But in a few seconds, Cade cleared his throat, bringing her attention back to him. "There is one more thing you and I need to discuss."

His sudden nervousness didn't fit with the straightforward conversation they were having and she tensed. "What?"

"Nick and Maggie think you should live with me at the ranch."

Positive he was joking, she laughed. "Right."

"Hey, I don't want you to. But I figured I'd better tell you just in case it somehow gets back to you that I was supposed to ask, but didn't."

Confusion wrinkled her brow. "Why would they want me to live at your ranch? What would I do so far out in God's country?"

He peeked over at her, clearly relieved that she thought the idea as crazy as he did. "Exactly." But when he caught her gaze with his sincere brown eyes, her heart stuttered a bit in her chest. "I mean, I'm sure we could find a university nearby…but you're probably eager to get on with your life."

She did want to get on with her life. She truly did. But something about this man called to her. It was more than sexual attraction. More than empathy for his loss and his suffering. A click of connection sparked in her every time she as much as looked at him.

But he didn't feel the same thing for her. And she had money now. Plans.

"I am eager to move on. I have to enroll in the next semester of classes." She paused. She'd already figured out she wasn't going back to her old school. There was no way she'd risk seeing Bill Baker. "Except I'm not quite sure what university I'll go to. With a whole country full of schools to choose from, it could take me months to figure out where I should go."

He skewered her with a look. "There is no perfect plan, Suzanne. But the bottom line to this is neither one of us wants you to live with me."

Considering how she'd begun to soften to him, he was right. It probably wasn't a good idea. She shook her head. "No. We don't."

"Okay, then don't overthink it."

She settled back in her seat, convinced they'd made the right choice. But the thought of living at his ranch lingered and then morphed into something she hadn't expected. It might not be a good idea to live with Cade, but she had to admit it would be nice to stay in Whiskey Springs. Nice to see if she and Amanda Mae could have the kind of close relationship she'd suspected from the day they'd met. Nice to see all the people she'd met at the diner again, make them friends.

Nicer still to have roots.

A place to raise her baby.

A home.

CHAPTER SIX

WHEN they finally arrived at Cade's private airstrip, he shoved Suzanne's diaper bag and suitcase into his truck while she buckled sleeping Mitzi's baby carrier in the rear seats and they headed to Whiskey Springs.

It was, at best, a fifteen-minute drive to her temporary apartment above the diner, but to Cade it seemed to take forever. First, he was eager to get to town. Because the land was flat, he could see Whiskey Springs off in the distance and tonight it had a weird red glow. Something he'd have to investigate once he got there. He couldn't believe one of the residents would be so foolish as to start a fire on a scorching hot June night in a drought. This time of the year, the land was sometimes so dry it was a wonder it didn't spontaneously combust. But there was no other explanation for the red glow. It had to be a fire.

Second, he needed to get away from the woman in the truck with him. He understood her desire to make her own way with her million dollars. To find a university, finish her degree, have a skill so she'd know she and her baby would never go hungry. Hell, he'd been equally determined to prove himself when he turned eighteen and his dad dumped five million dollars in his lap. He'd wanted the money—needed the money—but he'd wanted to be his own man, too. So he'd learned to invest, to build his dad's peace offering into a real pile of money he could use to make more money, and then more money and more money. Until his dad knew that even without the five-million head start, he would have made it.

So he and Suzanne were a lot alike. Enough alike that he realized he might be attracted to her for a little more than just her cute little butt. That's what had scared him the night he'd kissed her and why he'd been so determined to scare her off. He thanked God she'd decided to take her money and run. Otherwise, they might actually become friends.

He nearly snorted a laugh. Friends? If they

spent more than an hour alone, getting along, he'd have her in bed. And that wouldn't do either one of them any good.

Mitzi squeaked, then moaned slightly before she burst into genuine tears and everything inside of Cade stilled. Since meeting Gino, he was accustomed to squeaking and crying and even an occasional mess. Like spit-up. Having a baby brother had acclimated him to kids. Plus, it had taken some of the sting out of his own childlessness. True, he'd had a moment of regret when he'd heard about Whitney's pregnancy, but he'd sucked himself back out of that black hole. He would not ever have a child of his own. Period. He accepted that.

But hearing Mitzi, up close and personal, did the strangest things to his chest. It tightened. It sort of tingled. He wanted to turn around and comfort her.

"Shh! Mitzi, sweetie. We're almost there. Then Mama will take you out of that tight little car seat, kiss your sweet cheeks and tickle your belly."

Clearly not appeased, Mitzi only cried harder.

"Please, sweetie." This time Suzanne's voice held a note of pleading that clenched Cade's gut.

"Don't worry about her on my account."

Suzanne peeked at him. "The fussing's going to get worse the longer it takes us to get into town."

"I know. But we only have another five minutes." And the red glow hovering around the town got redder the closer they got. "She's a baby. She's been strapped in that seat for hours. I don't blame her for being uncomfortable."

Suzanne turned from trying to entertain Mitzi. "I know that and Mitzi knows that. I just didn't think you did."

"What? I look like some kind of baby monster?"

"No, but you can sometimes be a grouch."

He leveled his best watch-your-step look at her and realized he'd just proved her point. "Yeah, well, when it comes to kids I'm a lot more understanding than I am with adults."

The red skyline finally caught Suzanne's eye. She pointed out the windshield. "Is that normal?"

He shifted uncomfortably on the seat. "No."

"Oh, Lord."

He levered his foot on the gas pedal, pushing it to the floor. With Mitzi screaming and Suzanne's gaze glued straight ahead, Cade barreled the truck into town. He got only a third of the way down Main Street before Bob Patterson stopped him.

Dressed in the heavy-duty gear of a volunteer fireman, he motioned for Cade to lower his window.

Cade didn't waste time on greetings. "What's going on?"

"I'm sorry, Cade. It's the diner."

Suzanne gasped. "Oh, no."

Bob blew his breath out. "Total loss. Amanda Mae is beside herself."

Suzanne shoved her door open. "Is she down there?"

"Yeah, crying her heart out."

Cade watched in amazement as Suzanne blinked back her own tears. She jumped out of the truck and fumbled with the door of the extended cab and the catch on Mitzi's car seat.

Cade stopped her by grabbing her hand. "I'll take care of Mitzi. You go to Amanda Mae." He glanced out his window at Bob. "You take her down there."

"Yes, sir."

He caught Suzanne's gaze again. "And you stay with him. It won't do Amanda Mae any good to have you getting hurt rushing to her side."

With that, Suzanne scooted around the truck. Oddly, she did exactly as Cade wanted for once. She paused by Bob, who took her arm and directed her through the gathered crowd.

Mitzi squawked.

He opened the door and then the back door so he could reach in, unbuckle Mitzi and pull her out.

Holding her at eye level, he said, "All right. Here's the deal. Your mom had to rush down there, but we're going to take it a little slower. It's not going to help matters if you continue to squawk."

As if understanding, Mitzi stopped crying.

There. See? Everybody made too much of this whole parenting thing. Babies loved him because he was straightforward and honest with them. And he loved babies. If only because they didn't try to con you. The way he understood it, that particular bad behavior didn't present itself until junior high.

He settled Mitzi on his arm. But a thought occurred to him and he spun her around, holding her at eye level again. "Are we okay in the diaper area?"

She only looked at him. Her blue eyes as bright as her mom's. Her dark hair sticking up in all directions.

"What? I'm trying to see if you need a diaper. If you do, I'll handle it."

She still only looked at him.

Since she wasn't giving him any hint, his options were to check—which was not at all appealing—or take his chances. Hoisting her to his chest, he decided to take his chances.

She snuggled into his neck, nuzzling in as if she planned to go back to sleep—or as if she liked him, trusted him.

Wonderful feelings bubbled up inside him. But he told himself not to be ridiculous. Babies trusted anybody who kept them warm and dry.

Still, he couldn't stop himself from kissing her cheek before he began picking his way through the crowd. Most stepped aside as he ambled through. A few offered their regrets for his loss, since, technically, everything in town was his. But he didn't give a flying fig about the loss of one building. He'd created his plan to buy all the buildings in town so he could give people like Amanda Mae a break. He paid the taxes, took care of repairs, did renovations. A little town like Whiskey Springs didn't support its own pharmacy or diner or Laundromat. Hell, they barely supported a convenience store. So he'd bought them all, subsidized them, so the people who worked on his ranch or for the corporate offices of his oil company had the things they needed without having to drive forty miles to the closest city.

But though the building was his, everything inside that building had belonged to Amanda Mae, and he hoped to heaven she had insurance.

The closer he got, the more chaos surrounded him. Firemen worked diligently to ensure the fire didn't spread, but the diner was engulfed. Red flames leaped from the roof. The windows had already exploded out.

When Suzanne reached Amanda Mae, the diner proprietor was sobbing softly. Tears immediately sprang to Suzanne's eyes. She raced over to Amanda Mae, who was surrounded by townspeople. But the minute Suzanne appeared, she stepped away from them and threw herself into Suzanne's arms.

"I don't know what I'm going to do."

Suzanne stroked her hair. "I'm sure Cade will come up with something."

She shook her head fiercely. "No reason for Cade to care about my equipment and supplies. That's my doing."

"Well, insurance will—"

"I let my insurance lapse..."

All Suzanne could say was, "Oh."

Suddenly, Amanda Mae pulled away. "Oh, my gosh! I forgot. All your things were in the apartment."

Suzanne shook her head. "I didn't really have much."

"Which makes it all the worse that you lost it!"

"Let's not worry about me," Suzanne said, sliding her arm across Amanda Mae's shoulder. Inside, her heart was breaking. Not only had Amanda Mae lost everything, but she had no insurance. God only knew how Cade would handle this.

As if thinking him made him appear, he stepped through the crowd and walked over. Miraculously, Mitzi was sound asleep on his shoulder. The tears rimming her eyelids spilled over. It was probably the sadness of the moment that had her thinking this way, but she couldn't help seeing how adorable Mitzi looked with a man. A father.

Where had that come from? He'd warned her he was a terrible husband, not because he'd felt the need to unburden himself, but because they were attracted. He didn't want her to get ideas. She'd agreed. He would really be upset if he knew she'd seen him as a father for Mitzi.

Patting Mitzi's back, Cade walked over. "I'm sorry, Amanda Mae."

After blowing her nose, she batted a hand. "Don't worry about me. I think this might be the good Lord's way of telling me it's time to retire."

Suzanne gasped, but Cade said, "You're too ornery to retire. You need the diner. It's your life-line to the people of this town. I've got another building—"

"I don't want another building." Fresh tears sprouted in Amanda Mae's eyes. "I didn't have insurance, so I don't have the money to buy all new equipment. I'm old. I'm tired. I can't start from scratch."

"I have money."

The words popped out of Suzanne's mouth before the thought even fully formed in her head.

"It'll take a hundred thousand dollars at least just for the kitchen. Then there's the dining room. I'd need booths, tables, chairs, plates, cups—" She ran her fingers through her hair. "And supplies. Every piece of meat, every jar of mayonnaise, every egg is gone."

"I've got money to replace it all," Suzanne said, her voice slowing down as she really thought this through. She'd wanted to finish her degree, but she could delay that. Especially for a friend. Plus, if she invested most of her money in the diner, she could also work there. Except not as a waitress, but a partner.

"We'll be partners."

Amanda Mae blinked. "Partners?"

"I'll put up whatever it takes for new equipment, etcetera. You provide the expertise."

Amanda Mae sniffed.

"Cade's said he's got a building—"

"Yeah, but where are you gonna live? Your apartment's gone."

She glanced over at Cade. This was the part where it got tricky. He'd said his family wanted her to live with him. But in the plane they'd more or less decided that was a bad idea. Still, Amanda Mae needed her and she didn't so much want to finish school as she wanted a job. A place. Some security. Surely she could find an apartment once everything settled down with the diner. She'd only need to stay with him a week or so...

"Cade's brother wants me to live at his ranch."

Cade's mouth dropped open in dismay.

Amanda Mae gasped. "You can't give me your money and go live with Cade!"

"Sure I can. Cade and his brothers gave me a holding fee to buy my shares of their father's company's stock. And they were generous." She pressed her hand to her chest. "I can afford to do this."

Cade's deep voice drifted into their conversation. "Suzanne, can I talk to you for a second?"

Suzanne faced Cade with a hopeful smile. "Sure."

He dragged her away from Amanda Mae, who was immediately swallowed up in the comforting arms of the townspeople again.

"I thought the plan was to go find a school and finish your degree?"

"Look, I know what's really bugging you is that I told Amanda Mae I would stay with you. But I only said that so she wouldn't worry about me for the next few days. I won't stay with you long. As soon as we get the new diner started, I'll find a place and move out."

He rolled his eyes to the heavens as if seeking strength. "Suzanne, this is going to be a lot of work."

"I know, but I want to work. I also want to do this." She glanced back at the diner owner. "Do you know that in one month of being virtually homeless while I tried to figure out what to do, Amanda Mae was the only person who helped me?"

He sucked in a breath, patted Mitzi's back. "No."

"Even you ushered me out of town, suggesting that I go to the next town over for a hotel room."

He looked away.

"Nobody saw that I was struggling, putting up a good front but drowning, except Amanda Mae."

She caught his arm to get his attention, but sparks of electricity crackled up his biceps. And Cade knew exactly why it was a bad idea for them to live together.

Still, Suzanne kept talking as if nothing were amiss. "This is my chance to pay her back. I want it."

He squeezed his eyes shut. Technically, what she was suggesting made perfect sense. Plus, it would appease his brothers. But he knew in real life it was going to be a disaster.

Why did he have to be so attracted to this woman? What was it about her that made him forget that he wasn't interested? Because even if he was looking for a woman in his life, this particular woman needed a husband and a father for her baby. And he'd vowed he'd never marry again. Didn't his hormones realize he could not be a husband? He could not hurt another woman.

"Come on. It won't be so bad to have me and Mitzi around. Look how you like her."

His heart turned over in his chest. He did like Mitzi. In a matter of a few days, he'd come to adore this baby girl. But that was actually another problem. He'd be with this child twenty-four-hours-a-day some days. He'd grow attached. Maybe long for something he couldn't have. His own kids. His well-ordered life would turn into chaos. Not because a child made a mess of things, but because he'd remember those plans, those dreams he'd had with Ashley. A houseful of kids. Christmas Eves beside a fireplace with little girls and boys wide-eyed with expectation. Little League. Dance lessons. Being a proud papa in the audience when *his* little girl danced a solo.

He swallowed.

Those dreams were gone.

And this child would only make him long for things he couldn't have. She'd already more than halfway stolen his heart. Her pretty mom would make him think that maybe, just maybe, he should try again.

But that wouldn't just be a betrayal of Ashley. It would be a betrayal of Suzanne. He couldn't ever love as completely, as wondrously, as innocently as he'd loved Ashley. And anything less would be cheating Suzanne.

He handed Mitzi to her mom. "You have two weeks." He turned to go, but faced her again. "And while you're at my house you keep the baby quiet."

"I thought you said you didn't mind her fussing—"

"Driving in a car with a baby and living with one are two different things. Especially since my office is in the house. Keep her quiet and out of my way."

CHAPTER SEVEN

AT TEN o'clock that night, Cade's mom volunteered to take the baby. Because his truck already had the car seat, he and Ginny decided to exchange vehicles. Suzanne listened to their discussion without comment as they walked down Main Street to Cade's truck and stopped at the driver's side door.

"Take Mitzi to the ranch and put her in the room with the crib."

Ginny raised one eyebrow in response, as if questioning that. But he said nothing, only handed her his keys.

She gave her keys to him, saying, "My SUV is on Third Street."

Buckling Mitzi into her car seat, Suzanne gasped. "Oh, my gosh! I forgot about my car. It could be toast!"

"Where'd you have it parked?"

"There weren't any spaces behind the diner, so I parked it about a block away."

Ginny winced. "You might be lucky."

Cade said, "We'll check up on it after the fire's out."

When Mitzi was settled, Ginny opened the driver's side door. "I'll see you when you're done here."

"I think it might be pointless to wait up. You might as well stretch out on the bed. We could be here all night."

Suzanne gave Mitzi one last kiss on the cheek. When she hesitated over the baby, Cade caught her elbow and pulled her away from the truck.

"She'll be fine with my mom. We need to make sure Amanda Mae is settled, and right now you seem to be the person she's listening to. *Partner.*"

She winced at his tone, but hustled with him over to Amanda Mae. At least three times the diner owner pulled herself together, then broke down and cried some more. When the fire was out, the firefighters told her they would stay behind to ensure no residual sparks reignited, but she should go home.

Cade and Suzanne walked her to her sister's house, where her niece Gloria met them at the door. Doc came by with something to help Amanda Mae sleep. Holding the two pills, she hugged Suzanne and Cade then excused herself to get a shower and go to bed.

Suzanne and Cade found her Mercedes, which, aside from a bit of soot, was fine. She drove him to his mom's SUV and then followed him to the ranch. In the echoing marble-floored foyer of his big house, he tossed his mom's keys to the cherrywood table beneath a huge mirror.

"Since my mom is in the suite I'd planned to give you, I'll show you to a room you can use tonight."

"I'd rather be by Mitzi."

"My mom's a light sleeper. She'll get up with Mitzi if she cries." He headed up the stairs. "But if it will make you feel any better, I'll put you in the suite beside hers."

"It would."

"Great."

She didn't miss the sarcasm in his voice. She knew he wasn't happy she'd told Amanda Mae she was staying at his ranch, but she didn't want Amanda Mae to worry. Plus, she would be out of his house as quickly as she could find an apartment. There was no reason for him to be snippy.

They walked the length of a long hall and he opened the door on a pretty blue suite for her.

"Thank you. It's lovely."

He said, "Peachy," then turned, took the three steps across the hall and opened the door.

"That's your room?"

"Yep. You're right across the hall."

Memories of their kiss on the beach trembled through her. Though she was absolutely positive he wanted nothing to do with her, she also knew they were attracted to each other. And though this bedroom was only for one night, the room he would put her into for the next week or so until she found her own place was only a few more feet down the hall. They weren't so close as to be able to hear the rustle of sheets, but they were close enough that, if temptation arose, either one of them could take a short walk to find the other.

A little crackle sparked through her blood-stream.

This was ridiculous. They didn't want to be attracted. Still, there was no denying chemistry. Look what they'd done on the beach. Shared a kiss so hot they could have raised fog off the ocean. It wasn't wise to tempt fate.

"Don't you have another room you can put me in?"

"Thought you wanted to be by the baby?"

"Don't you have another room to put me and the baby?"

He opened his door with a small shove of his shoulder. "Nope. That's the only one with a crib. I'm not running a day care here."

With that he stepped inside his room and closed the door. Foreboding rustled through her like the wind rustles through leaves before a storm, but she straightened her shoulders and went into her temporary suite.

He might be attracted, but he wasn't interested. Except maybe sexually. But neither she nor Cade would be stupid enough to play with fire.

Still, she intended to be out of his house long

before it became an issue. And while she was here she could simply downplay their attraction.

Tired from staying up past four, and without Mizti to wake her, Suzanne slept until nine o'clock the next morning. When she woke, she panicked until she remembered Cade's mom had Mitzi. She sprang out of bed to find them, but realized she had nothing to wear but the filthy, smoky clothes she'd taken off the night before when she'd showered.

After a quick search, she found a fluffy white robe in the closet, and, using the comb in her purse, she managed to tidy her hair.

But she didn't waste time on makeup. She raced from her room and knocked on the door of the suite beside hers, the room Cade's mom had shared with Mitzi. But no one answered. Realizing they were probably already up and about, she ran down the wide spiral staircase, through the echoing marble foyer and to the hall, where she stopped.

She had no idea where Ginny and Mitzi were. The house was huge and it wasn't the only place they could be. There were barns, stables, a swimming pool, ponds. They could be anywhere.

Still, going to the only room she knew—the big office where she'd had her fateful conversation with Cade—didn't seem wise.

Except, he'd probably know where his mother was with Mitzi.

With a deep breath, she strode to the office and found him sitting behind the massive desk. Color suddenly warmed her cheeks. Not only did she remember what he'd been planning the last time they were in this room, but also she was practically naked beneath this robe. And he would know that.

This was not the way to downplay their attraction.

A dark-haired man in a suit sat on one of the chairs in front of the desk. Seeing her, he rose.

Cade rose, too. His eyes made a quick trip down her robe-covered body. "Suzanne."

She clutched the collar more tightly together. "Where is everybody?"

"If you mean Mitzi," Cade said, pretending great interest in something on his desk, as if

SUSAN MEIER

using his search as a way to keep his eyes off her, "my mom is feeding her breakfast on the patio by the pool."

She turned to race away, but Cade stopped her. "Hey, before you go, I want you to meet Eric."

She stopped, faced them again. "Eric?"

The young man in the dark suit nodded slightly. "Nice to meet you, ma'am."

"Eric is my personal assistant. I just gave him the rundown on your situation. He'll lead the search for accounts your grandmother might have set up for you that you don't know about."

She'd forgotten about that. "Oh."

"You authorized it."

She swallowed. "Yes. I remember."

"Don't scowl as if you've made a deal with the devil. Using my staff is just a way to save you some money." His voice shifted, changed, and laughter filled it as he said, "Money which you need, since you're now partner in a restaurant."

"Diner," Suzanne corrected, straightening her spine. Did he think she was going to bail? Or, worse, did he think she and Amanda Mae were going to fail? "And I'm fine with the promises I made last night."

"Then you'd better get a hitch in your get-along because I'm meeting Amanda Mae in an hour to talk specifics about a lease for the new building."

"An hour?"

"And it takes fifteen minutes to get into town." He sat behind the desk again, pointed at her robe. "By the way, I had someone get the suitcase you took to New York from the truck. It should be outside your bedroom door by now."

Suzanne spun around and headed upstairs. She dressed in jeans and a clean T-shirt then ran to the patio, where she found Ginny sitting at an umbrella-covered table with Mitzi beside her in the high chair.

Shielding her eyes from the sun with one hand, Ginny said, "Cade told me the two of you are going into town."

"Yes. We're meeting with Amanda Mae to talk about a lease for the new diner." Suzanne pulled Mitzi out of the high chair, hugged her and kissed her. "Hey, baby. Your mama's here now."

Drinking deeply of Mitzi's freshly bathed baby

scent, she let her gaze fall on the high chair and
her brow furrowed in confusion. Why would a
single man have a room with a crib and a high
chair?

Then she remembered Cade had a half brother.
Gino. The little boy wasn't Darius and Whitney's
son. But a half brother.

She hugged her baby again. "Oh, gosh. I missed
you."

Ginny laughed. "She missed you, too. She had
a screaming fit at about five this morning."

"Why didn't you get me?"

"Because we were fine. And you'd probably
just gotten to bed. She took a bottle. I sang her a
lullaby and she went right back to sleep."

Reaching over, Ginny tweaked Mitzi's cheek.
"You are a precious little princess, aren't you?"

Mitzi giggled.

Surprised, Suzanne caught Ginny's gaze. "She
likes you."

"She adores me and we will be fine all day
without you."

"All day?"

"You're going into town, remember?"

"Seeing the building and signing the lease shouldn't take more than two hours."

"Honey, there'll be insurance reports for Cade's insurance claim and investigators to deal with. Not to mention an internet search for the new equipment and then there's the time you'll spend with Cade and his lawyer."

She bit her lower lip. "I'd better get going."

She handed the baby back to Cade's mom, but before she could pull away, Ginny caught her hand. "You've never really left her for a whole day before, have you?"

She shook her head.

"We're fine." Ginny's voice softened. "Seriously. This is like a playdate for me, too."

Suzanne laughed and said, "Thanks," before she walked into the house again. Today she couldn't take Mitzi with her. But pretty soon she would be able to. She already knew Amanda Mae didn't mind having Mitzi in a swing nearby. Plus, as half owner of her own business, she called the shots.

Realizing that if the Andreas brothers had given her a job she would have had to leave her baby like this every morning, she raced up the stairs, grateful that her initial plan had failed.

Maybe she wasn't a jinx after all? Things might go wrong in her life, but good things always seemed to come of them. Her affair with the wrong man had produced a beautiful baby. The Andreas brothers' decision to give her a holding fee for the purchase of her stock rather than a job had resulted in her becoming a business owner.

A business owner!

She had a place.

She belonged somewhere.

Cade kept the meeting at his lawyer's office cool and professional. Amazingly, when it came time to make any decisions, Amanda Mae deferred to Suzanne. At first, Suzanne hesitated. Then Cade watched something shift in her pretty lilac-colored eyes. Her shoulders straightened imperceptibly, as if she'd realized she had to be the stronger partner in her deal with Amanda Mae while she recovered from the shock of losing her business.

As a professional negotiator Cade could have

balked over some of Suzanne's suggestions, but as an Andreas brother his priorities were different. He sent his lawyer a quiet signal that whatever Suzanne and Amanda Mae wanted, it was to be done—including that Cade would pay for the construction to turn the empty building into a diner.

Let Nick tell him he wasn't taking care of Andreas family business now. He'd all but handed Suzanne and Amanda Mae a sparkling new building. And—God help him—she was living with him. Just as Nick and Maggie wanted.

They returned to the ranch about three that afternoon and Suzanne headed upstairs to see Mitzi. He didn't follow her. Spending the day watching her eyes light with joy every time he met one of her conditions had turned his nervous system inside out. She glowed as she took the reins of her partnership with Amanda Mae. And every time she grew stronger, more confident, his chest tightened with a strange kind of happiness. Gooey, sappy, it spread from his chest and made him want to strut with pride for being able to help her.

It was just wrong.

Wrong.

He had no intention of getting close to her even though she was about to live with him for the next few weeks while she apartment or house hunted.

Knowing she could find his mom and Mitzi on her own, he walked back to the office where Eric was using his laptop for the search of assets.

"Anything?"

"Nothing so far. Even though I have her social security number, I hit the wall with the banks. I need to have Suzanne sign some releases. Then I'll go to the banks Martha Caldwell used most often, releases in hand, and we'll see what's what."

He fell to the sofa. "Sounds like a plan." But after only ten minutes of listening to Eric catch him up on things that had happened that day, he began to twitch, and he realized he was listening for Suzanne. Had she found the baby? Was the baby all right? Had his mom been okay watching her all day?

He sighed and hoisted himself off the couch.

Convinced it was the good host in him that was making him feel odd that he'd simply walked away from his guest, he headed out of the office. Damn his mother for drilling manners into him.

"I've gotta go check on Suzanne."

Eric grinned stupidly. "Sure. Fine. The rest of this can wait."

He nearly sighed again. Did *everybody* think he had a crush on Suzanne?

Taking the steps two at a time, he scowled. Of course they did. Because he was acting like a ninny about her. And after that earth-shattering kiss he might as well admit it. He *did* have a crush on Suzanne. A stupid crush. *Crush.* Infatuation. Not serious emotional attachment. They hadn't known each other long enough for him to have anything more than a sexual attraction. Sure, he'd realized they had something in common when he recognized her desire to make something of herself matched his own, but that was just one thing. There were too many good reasons to stay away from her to fall victim to an itty-bitty attraction.

Of course, there was the weird happy feeling he'd gotten watching her that day….

He scowled again. Seriously. Was even he going to question himself?

When he reached her door, he knocked twice. Knowing there was a small sitting room before the bedroom—so he wouldn't inadvertently catch her naked, but also she might not hear his knock—he turned the knob and opened the door.

Suzanne was halfway to the door, smiling from ear to ear. "Hey."

"Hey." He nodded at the baby she held. "Everything okay?"

"Yeah. She's great." She hugged Mitzi to her. "She loves your mom."

He hovered in the doorway. "Room okay?"

"It's lovely. Perfect." She glanced around at the comfy yellow sofa draped with a white angora afghan, the big-screen TV that could be hidden in the cherrywood armoire, the plush Persian rug on the floor grounding the grouping. "Actually, it's huge. My grandmother had some fancy suites, but this one is spectacular. That bathroom is to die for. And a baby bath? Whoever thought of that was just a genius."

He leaned against the doorjamb, hating the male pride that bubbled up in him at seeing how happy she was, and pretending he didn't feel it. "Yeah, it's nice."

"It's like the nursery is part of the suite." She frowned and gave him a puzzled look. "Do you sleep in here when Gino is here with you?" Her frown deepened. "Oh, wait. He has a nanny who probably sleeps here.…" She stopped again. "Gino's only two and this house is older than two years old." She glanced around, as if disoriented. "Was Gino even born when you built this house?"

He cleared his throat. "No. Putting a nursery in was just a commonsense thing at the time. If you're okay, I'm going to go back to Eric. We have tons of work to do. I eat at seven. If you want to join me, fine. If you want to eat sooner or later just tell the cook."

With that he left, cursing himself for being an idiot. Suzanne was a smart woman, who, as her confidence grew, was getting smarter by the minute. He could not have a crush on her. She'd figure it out…and then what? They'd be awkward around each other; that's what.

She had to live here for at least two weeks— maybe longer if she decided to buy a house and had to wait to take possession. He could not let her realize he was beginning to like her. So he had to get rid of the crush. Dismiss it. Pretend it had never happened. Because it was foolish. Ridiculous.

He was better than this, smarter than this, stronger than to fall victim to some idiotic crush.

Suzanne joined him for dinner that night, but Mitzi was fussy so she didn't get through the salad before she had to take the baby and run. Cade alerted the staff and finished his meal, but with every course he got more and more antsy. Mitzi wasn't a fusser. What if there was something wrong?

Telling himself he was simply concerned, he tossed his napkin to the table and made his way to Suzanne's suite. He hesitated. But knowing he wasn't about to walk away, he rolled his eyes and knocked on the door. If he didn't do this now, he'd just come up again later. Might as well indulge his curiosity and get it over with.

Within seconds Suzanne answered, holding naked Mitzi, who was wrapped in a terry cloth blanket.

"Everything okay?"

"Everything's fine." She turned and headed for the nursery. "Mitzi's a baby. She doesn't believe in anybody's schedule but her own. Right now she wants a bath and to go to bed. I don't get a say in it."

Following her into the bright green room with a matching white crib and changing table, and his mother's old oak rocker, he grunted. "What's with the blanket?"

"You mean the towel? Would you hold a naked baby without some protection against an accident?"

He laughed.

She paused and nudged her head in the direction of the baby's bathroom. "Come on. I'm serious. We have only seconds here before she does something we could potentially regret."

He followed. Slowly. For a guy who was determined not to have a crush on this woman, following her was equal parts of smart and stupid. It was stupid because every second he spent in her presence meant possible discovery. But smart because there was no room in this house that reminded him of his thwarted life plan with Ashley more than this suite. And maybe he needed a reminder of what a man was really supposed to feel for a woman. This sexual thing he had going for Suzanne was only part of a relationship. It would be wrong to make a fool of himself over a crush that was based on very little more than the fact that she had a hot little body.

His heart sort of hiccuped when he entered the bathroom that had been built off the nursery of the master suite—the bathroom his wife had designed—and everything fell into place in his head again. This room had been built for his babies. Having a stranger use it was a potent reminder that he'd never have a child. Especially not with Suzanne. Because he didn't love her. He *wouldn't* love her. He'd never again love the way he'd loved Ashley and he hadn't been a good husband to her, so how could he expect he'd treat Suzanne any better? She deserved more.

She *did* deserve more. She was a nice woman who had a baby who needed a daddy. Not some jaded old cowboy.

Suzanne lowered Mitzi into the waist-high baby tub that had been installed beside the sink. "I'm telling you, this place is a mother's dream."

Happiness swam through him at her praise, but at least this time he understood it. It wasn't wrong to be glad to see the bathroom put to good use. It was pragmatic. For the past two years he'd felt this part of his house was a waste. It was good to see a baby in the tub. Good to see the well-designed space making a mom happy.

Mitzi splashed in the water.

Suzanne gently tweaked her nose. "You love this, don't you?"

He cleared his throat. Now that he had his priorities straight, he could actually converse with her without feeling like his hormones were going to take him down all the wrong roads.

"Gino loves a bath, too."

"Oh, so you've bathed him here!"

"Actually, he's never even been to Texas, let alone to the house. I've had the honor of bathing him when I visit him in Montauk."

She laughed. "Ah, building memories with your little brother."

"That's what Whitney and Darius call it. I call it more like survival of the fittest."

"He's a splasher?"

"Yeah, he is."

She ran a small pink sponge along Mitzi's body as the baby slapped her hands in the water and babbled, not paying any attention to her mom. It seemed Suzanne was bathing the baby without Mitzi noticing.

Cade smiled. This was good. Really good. The little reminder that Suzanne deserved better than him seemed to have turned off all his unwanted feelings. He only felt positive, happy things.

He pushed away from the door frame. "Well, if you don't need anything…"

She peeked back at him. "We don't. We're fine."

"Okay, then I've got to catch up on the rest of what I missed today."

"Eric is still here?"

"No. He goes home at six. Sharp. Every day. He'll come back if I want him to. He'll work seven days a week if I need him to. But he's got a big dumb dog who has to be let out to pee at six-fifteen."

Suzanne laughed. The sound filled the bathroom like music. "That's adorable."

Panic fluttered in Cade's stomach. He wasn't supposed to love her laugh. "Dog's ugly as sin."

She shook her head and went back to rinsing Mitzi. "Those are the best."

He swallowed. Sucked in a breath. Reminded himself that getting involved with her would be cheating her, so he wasn't allowed to have these feelings.

It didn't work. One glance at her bathing the baby and the fluttery feeling in his stomach intensified.

So maybe it was time to suck it up and spend a few minutes talking, so he could grow accustomed to her voice, her laugh…everything. Then there'd be nothing new about her to resurrect emotions he didn't want to have.

"He named the damned thing Ostentatious."

For that Suzanne turned and grinned at him. "Eric named his dog Ostentatious?"

There. See? That wasn't so hard.

"He says the dog always makes a grand entrance, but I'm guessing what he makes are big messes."

Satisfied that his crush was losing some of its power, he turned to go, but Suzanne said, "Cade?"

He stopped, faced her again.

"Thanks. I know you did me and Amanda Mae some favors today."

He grunted. He had billions of dollars, using a few of those dollars to make sure two women got a chance with a new business shouldn't feel like a favor. It should be common sense. So why had his chest just swelled with pride once more?

"Don't mention it."

She smiled. And his heart did a silly flip-flop.

Damn it! The crush was still very firmly in place.

It looked like he had two choices. Option one? Ignore her. Now that their business was done and he knew her suite was adequate, he didn't even have to be in the same room with her.

Option two? Spend so much time with her that she stopped being special. Attractive. Unique. Fun.

Mitzi dropped the plastic ball she was gnawing on and it fell to the floor. Suzanne bent to scoop it up and Cade's eyes followed the smooth flow of her back and the rounding of her bottom as she reached to retrieve it.

He turned and scooted away.

For now, ignoring seemed like the better plan.

Though Cade avoided Suzanne all day Wednesday, the pull that night was too strong to defy. Still, he'd refused to go to her room. Instead, he asked Mrs. Reynolds, his house manager, if Suzanne had eaten.

"Miss Suzanne and Miss Mitzi ate around five-thirty. Mrs. Granger made a special pudding for Mitzi, which the baby gobbled up." She laughed lightly. "Then they played by the pool for an hour before retiring to their suite."

Hearing that stodgy Mrs. Reynolds hadn't been able to resist watching them either, Cade didn't feel nearly so foolish when he had to fight himself to keep from climbing the stairs to check on them.

What was it about babies and new moms that brought out the protective instincts?

God only knew. Not only were Nick and Maggie overly concerned about her, but his staff also had it bad. Mrs. Reynolds kept tabs on her. The cook made special food for them. If Eric started acting all sappy and mushy, Cade would know his entire household had gone around the bend.

He forced himself to stay in the family room, playing video football for two hours, absolutely positive Suzanne and baby would be asleep by the time he went to his room. But when he walked upstairs, the door to Suzanne's suite was slightly ajar.

He sighed.

Don't do it! Do not check on her! Every person on the staff has checked on her. Your own mother called to be sure they were okay. They are okay. You do not need to check!

Of their own volition, his feet wandered to her door. His knuckles tapped twice. The door creaked open a bit more, and there were Suzanne and Mitzi watching TV.

"Hey."

"Hey!" Suzanne rose from the sofa, bringing Mitzi up with her. "You have some timing. Last night you hit bath time. Tonight I'm just about to feed her a bottle and rock her to sleep."

"I was only going to ask how things went today with Amanda Mae. I'm guessing the shock has worn off and reality is setting in. I wanted to make sure you were dealing okay." How he'd come up with such a reasonable explanation for his presence on such short notice, Cade didn't know. But he was proud of himself. "Seeing as how you're busy, I'll go."

"No." She motioned him to follow her. "I can talk while I'm feeding her."

"Won't that defeat the purpose?"

"What purpose?"

"Aren't you trying to get her to fall asleep?"

"She's already dead on her feet. Once she starts

drinking her bottle, there won't be enough noise on the planet to keep her awake. One conversation won't bother her."

They talked about Amanda Mae while Mitzi guzzled her milk. She burped, then Suzanne let her have the bottle again. This time, she drank slower. Her eyelids drooped until she fell asleep.

When Suzanne glanced up, Cade was staring longingly at Mitzi.

The whole situation confused her. She knew Cade was attracted to her, but didn't want to be. His way of dealing with her seemed to be ignoring her. She'd decided that was as good a plan as any and she'd given him a wide berth. But this was the second night that he'd come into their suite.

To see Mitzi.

He'd told her that he wanted her to keep the baby out of his way, but he was the one who kept finding them because he clearly liked the baby. Which was so cute she couldn't really fault him for it.

"Wanna lay her in the crib?"

He caught her gaze. "I'll wake her."

"I told you. She's a heavy sleeper."

He swallowed.

Suzanne saw such raw emotion, such raw pain in his eyes that things fell into place for her. "You built this suite of rooms for yourself and your wife, didn't you?"

"It doesn't matter."

"Sure it does. I don't think you get this, but I can see you're drawn to Mitzi...drawn here. To this suite. I think because you're curious."

He turned away. "A bit."

"There's no shame in that."

He snorted a laugh. "Suzanne, let it go."

"No. Just give in to the feelings. Everybody loves a sweet baby and Mitzi's one of the sweetest. Why don't you let yourself admit you enjoy having a baby around?"

This time, when he faced her he was not laughing. "Let...it...go."

She laid Mitzi in her crib and walked over to Cade. "You think you scare me?" She snickered. "Seriously. Only a little over a week ago, I was facing the possibility of sleeping in my car.

You're going to have to do a little better than scowl."

"Okay, how about this?" He stepped closer, so close she could feel the heat of his body. "The reason I keep coming in here is because I have a crush on you."

She blinked. "What?"

"A crush. The hots. Call it what you want but I'd love to sleep with you."

She stepped back. Cleared her throat. She already knew that. He'd warned her off the night he'd kissed her. She just didn't think discussing it would do either of them any good. Still, she had to say something. "So you're telling me you're not coming in to see Mitzi?"

"No. I'm telling you that everything in my well-ordered life has been tossed in the air because of you." He turned away. Ran his fingers through his thick dark hair, spiking it. Then he spun to face her again. "I accepted my wife's death. I accepted that I'd never have kids. That my fate was to take care of my town. The people. And then you popped up and now everything's confused."

Suzanne frowned, backtracking to the most important thing he'd buried in his rant. "You can't have kids?"

"Don't know. We'd just begun tests to see why Ashley hadn't gotten pregnant in eight years of marriage when we found her cancer." He turned away. "Never seemed to be a reason to get myself tested after that."

"So you might actually be able to have kids?"

He shrugged. "Maybe."

"So don't torture yourself. Go get tested."

He spun to face her. "I think you're missing the big picture here. It doesn't matter. I was a bad husband. I'm not going to remarry. And I'm certainly not going to have kids with no mama."

"Why does that makes you mad at me?"

He took her chin, lifted her face until she caught his gaze. "I want to look at you only as somebody to sleep with. Then I could deal with you. Then I could get you in my bed or decide against it."

Her eyebrow arched skeptically. "I have no say."

He laughed softly. "If I decided I wanted you in my bed you would be there."

His tone made her swallow.

"But you have a baby. A little girl who reminds me how much I wanted to be a dad. To have sons. Boys to teach. Children to leave my legacy. And I'm not clear about anything anymore. Ashley was the love of my life. The woman I wanted to be the mother of my children. Without her, these rooms aren't supposed to tempt me."

"Maybe it's not the room." She didn't know how she got so bold, but the answer seemed glaringly easy to her. She stepped closer, mimicking his movement when he'd tried to intimidate her, showing him she wasn't afraid. "Maybe it's the situation. Since I'm as tempted by you as you are by me, then I don't see your problem."

He gaped at her. "I told you. I was a crappy husband."

That made her laugh. "You know what? I'm starting to think that's just an excuse. You're a nice guy. I see it every day. You bought a whole town so nobody would have to pay property taxes. You gave me and Amanda Mae more than a couple of breaks on our deal and you won't one-up your brothers and buy my stock. Face it, Cade. You're a nice guy."

He took a step closer, putting them so close they were just about touching. "You wanna test that, little girl?"

Her voice shook the tiniest bit when she said, "Yes," because she'd seen his kindnesses not just to her but to Amanda Mae, and his brothers. And he liked Mitzi. Wanted to be a dad. No matter how he saw himself, he was a good guy. He might have been a crappy husband to his wife, but it appeared her death had changed him. "I like you and you like me. Why shouldn't we do something about how we feel?"

"Because I'm being kind to you. Smart in the way I treat you."

"What if I don't want you to be smart?"

"You'd better. I don't intend to ever marry again and you need a husband. But if you push me, I might not be able to walk away from what you're offering."

Her breath stalled. No man had ever worried that he wouldn't be able to resist her. The mere thought sent a shiver of excitement down her spine, liquefied her knees. He stood so close that if she lifted her hand she could touch the stubble on his chin and cheeks. If she rose to her tiptoes she could kiss him.

Renewed boldness blossomed in her, along with an incredible need. What would it be like to make love with a man who desperately desired her?

Heaven?

Or maybe hell. He'd been very clear that he didn't intend to remarry. And just as he'd said, she needed more from a relationship than just sex. She wanted a husband. She couldn't get into a relationship with another man who didn't want forever. She needed someone to cherish her. Love her. Be her partner.

And maybe that was the real bottom line. She wanted a partner and he was offering a roll in the hay.

She stepped back, away from him. "You're right."

"Damn straight, I'm right."

He left quickly and Suzanne fell to her bed in dismay. Wonderful sensations still rumbled through her. Longing she'd never felt before. But fool me once, shame on you. Fool me twice, shame on me. She'd never again fall for a man who didn't want her.

Completely.

For good.

One Bill Baker was enough to last a lifetime.

CHAPTER EIGHT

THURSDAY morning as Suzanne drove up to the brand-new building that she and Amanda Mae had leased from Cade, everything about her new project suddenly became real for her.

She wasn't just a diner owner on paper. She was a diner owner for real. She sat in her car, staring at the building, with realizations knocking into each other like dominoes. By partnering with Amanda Mae she'd made decisions beyond offering money and agreeing to work. She was creating a life here, in this town. About to buy a house or find an apartment. About to interact with most of the people who lived in Whiskey Springs, if only because the diner was the only place to eat out. About to be an active resident of the town owned by Cade.

She laid her head on the steering wheel in

dismay. No wonder he had been so skittish, so agitated when she offered Amanda Mae a partnership. She had, without consciously deciding to, edged herself into his world.

She pressed her fingers to her temples, thinking it through and decided it was too late to call back her choices. She would simply have to learn to coexist with Cade.

And he'd have to learn to coexist with her.

Once she moved out of his house that should be more than possible. In the five days she'd worked as a waitress, he'd only come into the diner once. Surely, they could handle seeing each other once a week.

Shoving her shoulder against her car door, she got out, bounded into the building and discovered Amanda Mae was already inside.

"So, Joey, I want the kitchen to be right here."

A man Suzanne had never met jotted notes on a small pad of paper. Wearing a pair of brown coveralls and big work boots, he had to be a representative of one of the construction companies they'd chosen to ask for bids on the work required to turn an empty building into a diner.

Suzanne handed Amanda Mae a cup of coffee she'd picked up for her at the convenience store. "Is this one of the people who will be bidding on the renovations for the diner?"

The man looked up sharply, as if startled by Suzanne's question.

Amanda Mae popped the lid on her coffee. "He's the guy who'll actually be doing the work."

"I thought we'd agreed with Cade to go out for bids?"

"Yes, but my niece Jennifer's husband called last night saying Joey needed a job."

So many facts assaulted Suzanne that she didn't know which one to focus on. She understood Amanda Mae wasn't herself. Her entire world had gone up in smoke. She had a right to do things that were a little impulsive, even irrational. But they'd promised Cade they'd go out for bids, and after the conversation the night before, she did not want to cross him.

"But the agreement we signed with Cade—"

"It's irrelevant. I've seen Joey's work. He's the best in town. Cade will want the best."

Joey glanced at her and smiled sheepishly.

"I'm sure he will. But a bidding process—"

"Would be a waste of time since the guy who is the best is available." Amanda Mae turned to Joey. "So, how long will this take?"

"If I get the right crew, I can probably have this done in six weeks, maybe a month."

Amanda Mae gasped. "Six weeks! I can't go that long without an income."

In all the confusion, Suzanne had forgotten Amanda Mae needed money, so her rushing to get this moving faster made perfect sense. It was an argument she could give to Cade for why she'd broken their agreement. But more than that, Suzanne had a resolution for that problem, too.

She tapped Amanda Mae's arm. "Actually, I have an idea. In the city a lot of vendors provide breakfasts, lunches and snacks with carts. I thought we'd try our luck on the internet and see if we could find a cart for a reasonable price—"

"Or I could make you a small stand in front of the building here," Joey said. "No charge except for materials," he added, catching Suzanne's gaze, as if telling her he appreciated her letting him have the job. "And you could sell your things from that. Right outside the new building that you want customers to come to anyway."

Suzanne brightened. Not just because he was building it for nothing, but because he'd thought it through. Her confidence in the town's best builder grew. "That's great."

Amanda Mae was not quite so enthusiastic. "Yeah, but where are we going to cook the food?"

"We can't "cook" anything. We'll have to sell things like sandwiches that we can put together in the stand." She smiled at Amanda Mae. "Plus, I'm sure Mrs. Granger will let me use her kitchen to make a batch of cinnamon rolls every morning."

"Thought you said people would grow tired of them."

"Thought you said they wouldn't."

Amanda Mae sighed. "Okay."

Suzanne frowned. She might have agreed but her tone was dull, listless. Selling sandwiches from a stand outside the future diner was a fantastic idea. Amanda Mae should be jumping for joy. But she wasn't.

She glanced over at her partner, genuine concern squeezing her heart. If getting a substitute income from a sandwich stand hadn't perked her up, then Suzanne was going to have to think harder, be smarter, figure out ways to show her everything was going to work out.

They spent the rest of the day on the internet, using Gloria's laptop to begin looking for appliances, pots and pans and utensils for the diner, as well as supplies to equip their interim sandwich stand. Needing the things for the stand immediately, they ordered those items that day, and actually got an overnight delivery on most of them. It was expensive, but they would be back in business on Monday morning.

By the time Suzanne returned to the ranch, she was exhausted. But she knew she had to go to Cade's office to tell him she and Amanda Mae had hired a contractor.

With a deep breath for courage, she turned and walked down the hall. As always, Cade sat at the huge mahogany desk. When she knocked on his door frame, he glanced up.

"Yes?"

"We hired a contractor today."

Obviously annoyed, he put down his pen. "I thought you were going out for bids?"

"Joey Montinegro was available."

Cade picked up his pen again. "Oh, well, okay, then."

She took a step into his office. "I take it this guy is good?"

"The best."

"Thank goodness. Amanda Mae hired him this morning without telling me." She took another step into the room. She knew he wanted to avoid her, but he was the closest thing she had to a mentor and she was worried about Amanda Mae. Maybe he'd have some advice. "It was the weirdest thing. All day long she behaved oddly. Not like herself at all."

"She just lost her business. She's bound to have a few moody days."

"This went beyond moody. She seems really sad."

He sucked in a breath, but didn't look up. "She probably is. Creating a new diner and even having a partner are risky. She has to be worried that you guys could fail."

"She did mention not having an income until we open, but we're opening a sandwich stand right outside the new building. In a few days we'll have an income."

He busied himself with the work on his desk again. "Just give her some time. She'll rebound. People have nowhere else to go to eat but that diner. Soon she'll remember that and she'll be fine."

"Okay."

She waited for him to say something else, but he didn't. She tried to think of something else to say, anything to make her presence less awkward, and couldn't.

"Okay, then. I'll just go to my room and play with Mitzi."

She turned to go, but he said, "Suzanne?"

"Yes?"

"Will you be joining me for dinner?"

There wasn't one spark of anything in his dark eyes. No attraction. No recognition. No interest. He'd made up his mind, shored up his defenses. There'd be no more personal conversations, no getting to know each other. That was how he intended to coexist.

She could probably eat with him that night, but they'd be like two awkward strangers.

Her heart tweaked a little in disappointment, but deep down inside she knew it was for the best.

"No. I'll get something after I have Mitzi settled."

But Mitzi wouldn't settle that evening and the once-comfortable suite became unbearably cramped. Because she'd come home early, she'd already spent hours stuck in three rooms and suddenly she couldn't do it anymore. Glancing out the window, she saw a series of sidewalks and trails that led to stables and corrals off in the distance. She changed Mitzi's diaper, put on her scruffy tennis shoes and headed out for a walk.

Her "walk" ended up taking twenty minutes. By the time she arrived, she was breathless. Hindsight was always twenty-twenty, but she wished she'd thought far enough ahead not to sell her stroller in the big sale she'd had to earn money to pay off her grandmother's debts and taxes.

She paused, admiring the flower beds that skirted the thin concrete road, pleased that someone had taken the time to make the place pretty.

"See these?" she said to Mitzi. "They're petunias."

"Sweet Williams, up by the barn."

She glanced around, confused because she hadn't actually seen anybody as she walked up. She still didn't see anyone.

"Down here."

An older man, probably in his late fifties, rose from behind a huge flowering bush. "Jim Malloy. I'm foreman here. And you're—"

"Suzanne Caldwell." Because he'd pulled off his gloves, she extended her hand to shake his.

He shook his head and smiled broadly. "Hands are still a little too dirty for shaking. Can't say I recognize your name."

"I'm partnering with Amanda Mae Fisher on the diner. Cade's letting me live here."

"Ah, you're the heiress."

She snorted a laugh. "If that much gossip has

reached you here back at the barns, then you also know I didn't inherit any money."

"But you did get a big block of stock." He grinned. "Andreas Holdings stock. That probably put a burr in Cade's shorts."

She laughed. It wasn't funny that her being a shareholder of Andreas Holdings stock made Cade angry, but she loved the slang of this area. It provided a vivid, probably accurate picture of how Cade felt. She also loved the people of Whiskey Springs. Warm. Friendly. Genuine. Sometimes painfully honest. But she'd had so much dishonesty in her life lately that, even painful, the honesty was refreshing.

He pointed at Mitzi. "So who is this?"

She proudly presented her baby. "This is my daughter, Mitzi."

"Well, aren't you just the sweetest little thing?" He glanced at Suzanne again. "How old?"

"Six months...heading toward seven. It's really hard to keep up with baby ages. At first we counted in weeks, which was a dilly to try to figure out. Now counting months is nearly as hard."

"Yeah, it is." He glanced down at his dirty hands. "Wish I could hold her."

The regret in his voice hit Suzanne right in the heart. With his gray hair and kindly weathered face, he looked and acted like a well-loved grandfather. The sort of grandfather she'd always dreamed about but never had. She'd been so happy to have at least one living relative that she'd never told anyone about her secret longing for a granddad.

But suddenly that dream morphed and took a different shape. Because she had no relatives, her baby wouldn't ever have a grandmother or grandfather. No cousins. No aunts. No uncles. No father. She wished for a grandfather just like Jim Malloy for Mitzi, then stopped herself. She had to stop connecting herself to Cade. This guy was his ranch foreman. For both of their sakes, once she got a house in town, she'd have to stay away from anything connected to Cade.

"I guess I'd better get back. If Cade comes up to my room to say good-night, he might worry if I'm not there."

"You didn't tell him you were leaving the house?"

"No. I sneaked out. You could say he's really not happy to have me underfoot."

Jim peered over at her. "It's not like Cade to be unhappy about having a pretty girl around."

"We sort of bring out the worst in each other." Feeling odd talking about Cade with one of his employees, she changed the subject. "It doesn't matter." She nodded at the flowers at their feet. "By the way, I think it was a great idea to pretty up the area with flower beds."

He sighed, looked skyward. "It wasn't my idea. It was my daughter's." He caught her gaze. "I tend them for her now that she's gone."

It took a second, but only a second, for that to sink in. "You're Cade's wife's father? Ashley's dad?"

His eyes narrowed. "So he told you about her?"

She cleared her throat, made a mental note never to walk to the barns again and quietly said, "He spoke very highly of her. He loved her...I think he still does love her. She must have been a wonderful person."

"She was."

Suzanne saw tears fill his eyes and took a step back. "I should probably return to the house."

He said nothing, simply knelt down again and went back to weeding.

Walking beside flower beds that wound along a road that led almost to Cade's house, she suddenly understood why he couldn't consider another relationship. Reminders of his deceased wife were all around him…and so was her father. A father who'd never move on from the death of his daughter. A father who would mourn the loss forever.

A father who might also remind Cade he hadn't been such a wonderful husband.

The following Monday, Suzanne woke early, made her cinnamon rolls and headed for the sandwich stand. This was the day they would open for business. After stocking the stand on Friday and Saturday, she'd spent all day Sunday at the ranch, avoiding Cade, so it felt blissfully wonderful to have somewhere to go.

When she arrived, Amanda Mae was already

there. "Give me those beauties," she said, taking a tray of cinnamon rolls from Suzanne's hands. "People are lining up."

Suzanne laughed. "And you've been worried that we'd fail."

Amanda Mae sighed. "All right. I get it. I know I was a bit of trouble last week, but I'm okay now and we need to get selling. So I'll say I'm sorry I was a grouch and we can get to work."

She turned to leave but Suzanne caught her arm, refusing to let her go without really talking this out. "You weren't a grouch. You were concerned about the future. I understand. I've been through a loss or two myself. I'm guessing I was probably a little hard to get along with after my grandmother died. Maybe even when I first came to Whiskey Springs."

Amanda Mae chuckled. "So, we're even?"

Suzanne smiled. "I think we're better than even." But as Amanda Mae carried her tray of rolls to the stand, Suzanne said, "Actually, I could use your help with something else."

Setting the tray of rolls in the front of the display case so everyone could see them, Amanda Mae said, "What?"

"Finding someplace to live."

For that Amanda Mae turned around. "You're leaving Cade's?"

"I was only supposed to stay there until I found a place. But we've been so busy I haven't even started looking for a house or an apartment. Now I've got to get moving."

"You have any money?"

"They gave me a nice chunk of change to hold my stock. Lots of it went for diner equipment and things for this stand. Lots more is going for taxes. But I have a bit left. As long as I don't get carried away, I'll be fine."

"And pretty soon we should be making enough that we can both take a salary."

"Yeah. That's right. Pretty soon I'm going to get a salary!"

Amanda Mae laughed. "Okay, then I'll make a few calls."

Cade left the office that afternoon at three. He was tired of working, and one of the perks of being rich was that if he didn't feel like doing anything, he didn't have to.

He headed outside to the pool house, intending to change into trunks and enjoy what was left of the gorgeous day. The sky was blue. The sun was hot. And he owned a swimming pool he rarely used. So today was the day.

But when he stepped onto the patio, he found his mom and Mitzi. He'd almost forgotten about them.

He ambled over. "Hey."

His mom peered up at him over her sunglasses. "Hey. What are you doing out here?"

"Don't feel like working." He stooped down in front of Mitzi who sat in a pack-and-play under a huge umbrella. "How's it going for you today, kid?"

She gurgled a laugh.

"Does she go into the pool?"

"She loves the pool." She pointed to a small box past the pack-and-play. "See, she has two floaties and a turtle."

"What the devil is a turtle?"

"It's a one-piece suit that's a life jacket for a

baby. I saw one on the internet and couldn't resist buying it." She held up the garment that looked like it was stuffed with foam blocks. "See? It's padded enough and covers so much that it sort of looks like a tortoise shell when she puts it on."

He laughed. "Great. Give me two minutes to change and I'll take her in the pool with me."

"Actually, Cade, I'd appreciate if you could finish watching her for the day. I made dinner plans with Mary Louise Marks and I'd sort of like to slide by the beautician for a trim before I go."

Cade laughed. "Let me change into a suit and I'll give you your freedom."

He ran to the pool house and put on trunks. By the time he came out, his mom had not only stuffed Mitzi into the one-piece swimmer, she'd also gathered her things and was ready to go.

"You're not getting tired of this, are you?"

"No. But I have been neglecting the bookstore. Babysitting for Suzanne came up so quickly I never had time to look at my calendar. There may be more days I can't babysit."

Cade waved a hand in dismissal. "We have a

staff here. You don't need to be here every hour of every day. From now on, just come and go as you want. The staff and I will work it out."

"Thanks." She kissed his cheek then scampered off.

He carried Mitzi toward the shallow end of the pool. "You know that outfit makes you look fat, right?"

Mitzi giggled.

He grinned. "Finally, a woman who doesn't obsess about her weight."

Mitzi laughed again.

Cade waded into the pool, then, holding Mitzi under the arms, he skimmed her over the surface of the water.

She giggled with delight. A fluffy feeling invaded his chest. He let her dip a little deeper and she screeched.

He pulled her out of the pool and examined her face. "Is that good or bad?"

She giggled.

"Okay. Good."

He dipped her again. They played in the pool for at least an hour then Cade took her out and sat down with her on the chaise lounge. She was so small, so soft and so sweet. Part of him couldn't help longing to take care of her. To be the one to teach her to ride a pony. To be the one to teach her to swim. To be the one to pace the floor when she went on her first date.

But he couldn't. He knew he couldn't. Soon Suzanne would move out, taking Mitzi with her.

Still, he cuddled the baby closer. What was the harm in enjoying the few minutes or days he might get with her? None.

Mitzi fell asleep on his chest and he slid his arm over her, making sure she stayed put, before his own eyelids began to droop.

And that was how Suzanne found them. Her baby girl cuddled up to Cade, sleeping soundly. For several minutes she just stood staring at them, her own wishes and yearnings floating through her. It was so hard to believe Cade thought he was a bad person that at times like this she wanted to shake him silly and make him see he wasn't. But she also knew herself. She sometimes saw the good in people when there was none. And she couldn't be fooled a second time.

Still, he looked so cute with a baby. And Mitzi looked so cute with a daddy.

With a sigh of longing, she walked over to the chaise and as carefully as possible lifted Mitzi from his chest.

He immediately woke. "Hey—" He blinked, recognized who she was and said, "Sorry about that."

"What? I'm the one who should be sorry for not being here with my own child." She glanced around. "Where's your mom?"

"She had an appointment this afternoon. So I took over the job as babysitter."

Suzanne gasped. "I'm so sorry!"

He shifted on the chaise. "We have a staff. It's not like you're putting anybody out. In fact, my mom told me today she has a few things she needs to do at the bookstore and I told her not to worry. We'll handle Mitzi."

She caught his gaze. "You don't mind?"

He nonchalantly rose from the chaise. There was no way he'd let her see how much he'd enjoyed the afternoon. He didn't want her to get ideas again. He'd play this off as a duty. A task he could assign to his staff. "No. We'll be fine. You just go to work at your regular time and I'll instruct Mrs. Reynolds to be available if my mom needs her."

Wide-awake now, Mitzi squirmed. Full of energy she leaned toward the pool, screeching as if demanding to go back in.

Cade winced. "That's my fault. I let her play in the pool until she pooped out. Now that she's rested, it looks like she wants in again. Sorry."

But Suzanne laughed. "You're sorry you got time to take my little girl for a swim? Right about now I envy you."

She chuckled and headed for her suite, and he ran his hand down his face. She might envy him his free time, but he envied her more. Even with a job that took most of her day, a partner struggling to regain her footing and no home, Suzanne had everything he wanted.

CHAPTER NINE

THE following day, Suzanne came home to find Ginny with Mitzi as usual. Ginny told her about the dinner engagement and needing to go to the beautician and Cade's offer of staff to take care of the baby.

Grateful to both Ginny and Cade, Suzanne said, "Thanks."

But Ginny brushed off her thanks. "We love her, Suzanne. The staff actually groans when I come in and take her."

Confident that no one felt put-upon taking care of Mitzi, Suzanne didn't worry. The following two nights she came home to find Mrs. Reynolds with Mitzi. But the Saturday evening, when she returned home a little later than normal and a lot more tired because there had been an unexpected rush for sandwiches for quick suppers, Cade was walking down the foyer stairway with Mitzi. In spite of her exhaustion, she couldn't help noticing how adorable they looked. The gorgeous dark-haired man with the adorable dark-haired baby. They could be father and daughter.

Longing tightened her chest, twisted her heart. She knew it had to be exhaustion that caused that slip, so she ignored it. "Hey."

"You look like hell."

After fourteen hours making sandwiches, she probably did. She wanted desperately to toss her purse to the foyer table and collapse on the floor. Her second-best desire was to go upstairs, shower and collapse on the bed.

Instead, she clapped her hands to Mitzi. "Come to Mama."

Cade held her away. "I'm serious. You look like hell. When was the last time you slept?"

"Last night."

"Don't try to buffalo me. I know she gets up at night. And I know you set your alarm for five every morning to make cinnamon rolls. When do you sleep?"

The urge to collapse against him and whine

nearly overtook her. She'd been a spoiled college student when her grandmother died. Now suddenly she was a single mom, half owner of a diner, and she felt like she was drowning.

But he was not the person to tell. He didn't want to get involved with her. But his kindnesses to Mitzi sometimes had her forgetting that.

"I'm fine." Embarrassed, she took Mitzi from his arms. "I can be a mom and work. Millions of women do it." She shifted to the left, so she could walk around him up the stairs.

"Suzanne—"

She turned, tears pooled in her eyes. She wasn't just tired, she was beginning to see him in ways that weren't right. A father for her child. A confidant for herself. He might think he was a bad person but every day she saw evidence that he wasn't and she was beginning to like him. A lot.

"I'm sorry. I didn't mean to insult you. I was just saying I could keep Mitzi a while longer."

"I'm fine."

But she wasn't. She was tired and swimming in confusion. But she couldn't tell him that. She didn't want to get any closer to him than she already was, like him any more than she already did. And that's all talking would do. Make her like him even more than she already did.

Not wanting to spend another Sunday avoiding Cade, she packed Mitzi in her car. They took a long drive, and eventually drifted over to Amanda Mae's house. She made hot dogs on a grill and they sat on lounge chairs under a tree.

"So are you going to tell me what's bothering you?"

She couldn't really tell Amanda Mae she was exhausted. The woman was twenty years older than she was and not even slightly winded by the amount of work they were doing. Besides, this was her first job and they'd only been working a few weeks. Surely things would get better?

"Nothing. I'm fine."

"No, you're not." Amanda Mae studied her face for a second. "Okay, now I'm gonna go to meddling, but since we haven't been able to find you an apartment I think I know what's troubling you." She paused, sucked in a breath. "I've seen this thing that's been going on between you and Cade."

Suzanne stiffened. "There's nothing going on between me and Cade."

Amanda Mae laughed. "I saw your chemistry with the guy before you did." She laughed again. "Anyway, I'm guessing that has something to do with your sudden appearance at my house today."

Since that was the truth, she couldn't deny it. "Because I'm gone so much, he spends a lot of time with Mitzi." She swallowed. "He's awfully cute with her and she loves him." Her throat suddenly became unbearably tight, but she trudged on because it felt good to finally be able to admit some of this. "After I see them together, I get weird feelings. Like how he'd make a really good dad. But even though he likes me, he's said he doesn't want anything to do with me. So now, when we're both home, I feel like I have to hide from him."

Amanda Mae's face softened. "Oh, honey. Don't take it personally. He was so in love with Ashley. So young when he met her and so young when he married her. I don't think he even dated anybody else. After she died, he dated a bit for fun and company, but not looking to replace her. He can't replace her." She shook her head. "No, he *won't* replace her. And there's a bunch of us in town who respect that. But—" she sucked in a breath and caught Suzanne's hand "—that doesn't help you. Especially when we can't seem to find you an apartment so you can move into your own place."

"I'll figure something out."

Amanda Mae shook her head. "Actually, I've thought this through and I don't want you to stay in Whiskey Springs because of me. I appreciate you sticking by me through my sulk over losing the diner, but things are going well now. I ran the business myself before our partnership. I can run it again. If you think you need to go, go. Take a week, take a month, take a year. Just know that I'd like to see you come back." She shrugged. "You know. Be my partner. There's no man worth losing a friend over."

Suzanne's throat tightened even more. Amanda Mae might have run the diner, but she'd had help.

Waitresses. Busboys. The sandwich stand was a totally different animal and Suzanne couldn't abandon her. "Thanks, but I'll be fine."

Amanda Mae considered that. "And if you're not?"

"Then I'll take some time." She caught Amanda Mae's forearm. It had been so long since anybody really cared about her that she swallowed back a bucket of tears. "Thanks."

Amanda Mae groaned and batted a hand. "Don't go getting all mushy."

Suzanne laughed, as she fought her tears. She and Amanda Mae really had formed a bond. That was why she didn't want to leave. Whiskey Springs was the home she'd always wanted. Amanda Mae was quickly becoming the stand-in for her mom, who had died too young. The only fly in the ointment was her longing for a man who didn't want her.

It was dark when Suzanne returned home, but she felt better. Relaxed. But Wednesday night she was exhausted again. There was another rush on the stand just before supper time. Apparently, no one in Whiskey Springs felt like cooking on Wednesday and Saturday nights.

Done in, she melted onto the seat of her Mercedes, drove the fifteen minutes to Cade's ranch, rolled out of the car and went in search of her baby. When she found no one in the nursery, she groaned. She'd hoped only to have to walk up the stairs, bathe the baby, feed her and then shower herself before she could fall into bed.

But no such luck.

At the top of the stairs, she was so tired she considered folding herself into a ball and rolling down rather than walking. But she managed the steps, a trip to the kitchen—which was empty—a trip to the office—equally empty—and finally she found Cade and Mitzi in the pool.

"We just got in," Cade said as she walked across the patio to them.

"Oh. I was kind of hoping to take her upstairs and get her ready for bed."

"And I was thinking some time in the water might make her sleepy."

He was suddenly very knowledgeable about the baby, but she didn't have the energy to dwell on that or even out-and-out ask him why. Instead, she headed for the chaise lounge, hoping she didn't fall asleep while she waited for them to come out.

Cade played with the baby for another minute or two then he said, "Why don't you come in, too?"

"I don't have a suit."

"We have at least thirty in the cabana. They're all new. Once someone uses one, we tell them to take it home."

After standing out in the Texas sun for twelve hours, her sweaty body almost wept at the thought of diving into the cool water. But that would mean spending time with Cade—with both of them half-naked. Not wise. "I don't know."

Holding Mitzi securely with one hand, Cade skipped the other along the water, sending a cold spray over Suzanne. Sputtering, she bounced off the chaise.

"Hey!"

"Now, you're wet. No reason not to come in."

Sighing, and too tempted by the prospect of a refreshing dip to refuse, Suzanne walked into the

2

cabana. He'd made his feelings plain and she'd already decided not to be stupid. She might like him a little more every day. But he did not like her.

As Cade had said, there were plenty of swimming suits, all with tags. She found her size and cringed at the tiny bikinis. There was no way in hell she'd go prancing out to the pool in a little red two-piece number. She rummaged along the rack until she found a pretty aqua one-piece. It not only fit, it also covered everything but a spare inkling of cleavage.

It was fine.

Really.

A little self-conscious, she walked out of the pool house and ambled over.

Cade made a big deal out of not watching her walk to the pool. He admitted to a bit of disappointment that she'd chosen the one-piece suit, until he saw how pretty she looked. The color suited her dark hair and creamy skin. Plus, covered or not, her curves were very nicely outlined.

Still, knowing she was off-limits, he focused all

his attention on skimming Mitzi along the top of the water as Suzanne dived off the diving board.

When she surfaced, water ran from her hair along her shoulders down the crevice between her breasts. It was everything he could do to keep from staring. So he skimmed Mitzi along the water again, making her giggle, taking his attention away from Suzanne.

"Come on, baby. Want to come to Mama?"

Cade skipped her along the water, out of Suzanne's reach. "We're okay."

Mitzi giggled and Suzanne said, "I see that."

"We actually go to the pool every day."

"Really?"

Because her voice vibrated with concern, he added, "I love to swim, but laps can get boring. She gives me a reason to be out here."

Suzanne's eyes softened. Their pretty blue color always fascinated him but this evening's softness filled him with trepidation. He'd lured her out to the pool to relax because he'd been worried about her. Now he not only saw the flaw in his plan, he also remembered why he'd been ignoring her. She was gorgeous. And he was tempted.

"That's actually kind of cute."

Trying to bring back the light mood, he snorted in derision. "Yeah, well, don't go telling the people in town. I have a reputation to maintain."

She laughed and everything inside of Cade responded, except not out of attraction, out of something else, something stronger, something warmer. Pleasure. Though he knew he was skirting a dangerous line, something pushed him to keep going, to make her laugh again, to make her happy.

"I'm serious. Something like this gets out, every woman in a three-mile radius will be bringing her baby over."

She laughed, slid her hand through the water. "You'd love it."

His heart stumbled. His chest tightened. Lord, he loved it when she laughed. Groping for something to bring them back to normal, he said, "For about a day and a half. Then it would get old. Let's just let Mitzi benefit from this."

"Yeah. She deserves it." She skimmed her hand along the water again, suddenly avoiding his gaze. "I feel really bad that she doesn't have a daddy."

So did he, but he also knew the truth. Pretty girl like Suzanne wouldn't be alone long. Though that thought squeezed his chest even more, he softened his voice and said, "She will. Someday."

"I have every intention of being a good mom, a great mom. But I know what it's like not to have a daddy." She shrugged. "Or even a granddaddy. I know it's a longing she'll always have. I have to fix that."

He swallowed. "You will."

She finally glanced over at him. "I hope. Otherwise it will be the great failure of my life."

He sniffed a laugh, glad to be reminded of why she had to be off-limits for him. *His* great failure. "We all get a great failure in life. Why should you should be any different?"

"Because mine involves someone else. A baby who doesn't deserve to do without because I was a poor judge of character."

"And my wife didn't deserve to be the one to suffer because I spent so much time away." He shrugged. "Lots of life isn't fair." Knowing they'd already been over his feelings about his first marriage and not wanting to tread that path again, he changed the subject. "So how was work today?"

She didn't hesitate. "Exhausting. I had no idea fifty percent of the population of a small town could want sandwiches for supper every Wednesday."

"Your cash registers must be singing."

"Amanda Mae is in her glory."

He laughed. "But you're just tired."

"Don't make a big deal out of it. This diner is going to be the best thing that ever happened to me. Already, I'm making friends. I love this town. I love the people. I never would have met half of them had it not been for the diner."

He wanted to tell her that it wouldn't do any good to know everybody in town if she died from exhaustion. But he said nothing because a little voice inside him reminded him that her love of the town caused another complication for him. All this time he'd envisioned her being out of the picture once she left his house. Instead, he realized that exactly the opposite would happen. As she made friends, she would be invited to

barbecues, baptisms, weddings, swim parties…
everything he would be invited to.

She was in his life for good now. Permanently.

And he was going to have to watch when she
found the daddy she so desperately wanted for
Mitzi.

Because Cade agreed with Suzanne—her baby
did deserve a dad—he knew he couldn't be hang-
ing around, playing with her baby, trying to make
her smile, clouding the issue for her and himself.
So he avoided Suzanne after that and let Mrs.
Granger and Mrs. Reynolds care for the baby
when his mom couldn't.

But two Thursday later he still couldn't quite
put them out of his mind. He returned from a
meeting at the bank and walked back to his office
to find Eric happily occupied at his desk in the
room next to Cade's, and his messages neatly
stacked beside his phone. But he didn't care one
whit about returning those calls. The urge to find
Mitzi or drive into town to check on Suzanne was
so strong he had to fight himself to plop down
on his chair.

Then his phone rang.

Glancing at caller ID, he saw it was his brother, punched the button and said, "Hey, Nick."

"Hey, Cade. I've got you on speaker. Darius is with me in my office."

"What's up?"

"Maggie wants you to invite Suzanne to the wedding on Saturday."

"Are you serious?"

"Dead serious," Nick replied. "You're coming anyway. It shouldn't matter if you fly her over with you."

Cade groaned. After two weeks of not talking to her, he still thought about her way too often. Now they'd be alone for a three-hour plane ride. Then there was the twenty-minute drive in the limo to Nick's house. They'd be at the same table for lunch and dinner on Friday, as well as breakfast, lunch and dinner on Saturday. Not to mention the actual wedding itself. He wouldn't survive that.

"I'm not even sure what time I'm leaving."

"You can work that out with her," Nick said.

"Come on, Cade. Maggie likes Suzanne. She wants her there. She's afraid she's lonely."

"And Whitney thinks she needs family," Darius added. "After her visit here, Whitney had expected her to call and chat but she hasn't. So Whitney called her cell phone but she didn't answer."

"She's busy all day with Amanda Mae's diner."

There was a pause. "Amanda Mae's diner?"

"Suzanne made friends with Amanda Mae, the local diner owner. So when we saw the diner burning the day we got back from Montauk, she got caught up in the moment and offered Amanda Mae as much money as she needed to get the diner up and running again."

Another pause.

Cade slid his hand across the back of his neck. "I know you probably think this is insane, but she's busy and I know she's happy working at the diner—even if she is exhausted. Plus, because the apartment she was using also burned, she's forced to live with me until she can find a house or a condo."

"Well, that's something," Darius said. "But it

sounds like she could use a weekend off. Bring her to the wedding."

"Yeah," Nick said. "It's going to be great. Ceremony on the beach. Big reception afterward. She'll have fun."

"Plus," Darius chimed in, "Whitney will hound me to death if she thinks 'one of ours' is being left out. So bring her."

They talked only another minute before Darius and Nick clicked off. As Cade hung up the phone, the antsy, hungry feeling he usually had around Suzanne was superseded by real concern. He rose from his chair and paced to the window, scrubbing his hand across his mouth.

He couldn't stand to think of Suzanne as alone, but now that his family had forced him to see it, he realized she'd basically set it all out for him. Her mom had died. Her gram had died. Mitzi's father had dumped her.

She'd come to a town where she knew absolutely no one, looking for a job, and Amanda Mae had given her one. Now she and Amanda Mae were friends and she was also making friends with the locals. But he understood what concerned Maggie and Whitney because it suddenly concerned him, too. She had no family.

No one. She might have friends and customers and people to talk to on regular days but what about holidays? Days when the diner was closed? In the times when a person needed a family, she'd always be alone. That's what Whitney and Maggie sought to prevent.

He couldn't let his attraction to her stand in their way.

Suzanne was surprised to find Cade waiting for her in the front foyer when she returned to the ranch house that afternoon.

"You and I need to talk."

"Now? I haven't even seen Mitzi."

"She'll be fine with my mom for another few minutes."

Tired and sweaty from a day of selling sandwiches, cinnamon rolls and drinks, she wanted a shower and twenty minutes alone with her baby. But she knew determination when she saw it and right now it was written all over Cade's face.

"All right." She crossed her arms on her chest. "Let's get this over with."

"You're not going to the gallows."

"I know but I'm tired."

"Getting up at five-thirty to be in town by eight every day will do that to you."

She rolled her eyes. "Haven't we already been over this?"

He sighed. "All right. You're right. Let's just get to it. Nick and Maggie would like you to come to their wedding on Saturday."

Her heart stuttered. It was equal parts of wonderful and confusing to be invited to the wedding of people she barely knew.

"Please don't tell me you don't want to go."

"I do want to go." Desperately. She liked Whitney and Maggie. She'd thought they'd made a connection. True, she was making friends with people in town every day, but she had a different feeling around Maggie and Whitney. Almost like what she imagined having sisters would feel like.

"We're leaving Friday morning. We'll stay that night and Saturday night and return Sunday afternoon. Can you leave Amanda Mae alone Friday and Saturday?"

She chewed her lower lip. "I suppose she could get Gloria to help her at the stand."

"Good. You need a break."

She couldn't argue that.

Cade took a step closer. "You and Amanda Mae also need to work out a plan for this stand of yours. It might be time for a new schedule or maybe even time to hire an employee or two. You can't go on like this. You're exhausted."

He was the only person who seemed to care about that. Even Amanda Mae didn't see that by the end of every day she was dragging. The fact that he did, coupled with his nearness, caused her to swallow hard.

"I know neither one of you wants to be doling out money right now, but—" his voice softened unexpectedly "—you have to think of your health, Suzanne."

A shiver of attraction worked its way through her. He didn't seem to notice how close they were standing or that he was worried about her, being kind to her. It amazed her that he didn't see himself as a good person. Because ever since their trip to Montauk all she saw was goodness in him.

Unable to help herself, she looked up, caught his gaze. "We'll work something out."

"I hope so."

She smiled in response, and though he didn't return her smile, he did hold her gaze. Silence stretched between them. She thought about their time in the pool—when he looked so cute with Mitzi, when he talked to her about getting a daddy for Mitzi—and wondered how he couldn't see that she didn't want just anybody to be a father for her child. She wanted him.

She *did* want him. In spite of the way he kept warning her off, she was falling in love with him. And he'd also shown her signs that he liked her more than he wanted her to believe. Maybe even more than he let himself believe.

Which meant, if she wanted this, then maybe she'd have to make the first move.

She rolled to her tiptoes and brushed her lips over his. Need tingled through her, along with an amazing power. He hadn't moved. He barely breathed. But he also hadn't run, stepped back, told her no.

Her heart jumped to her throat. He was actually giving her a chance.

She rose a little higher on her tiptoes and, balancing herself with her hands on his shoulders, pressed her mouth to his.

She expected at least a bit of resistance, so when his mouth relaxed under hers and his hands dropped on her hips, a swell of feminine hunger shot through her. The time for pretense was over. He was everything she wanted and if he wanted her, she wasn't going to let him pretend otherwise. She deepened the kiss, but he quickly took control, opening his mouth over hers, forcing her to open hers to him.

Time spun out as his mouth seared hers in a hot, passionate kiss. Achy needs rose like wildflowers. Everything she knew or thought she knew about passion redefined itself in one blistering kiss. Her bones liquefied. Her blood shimmered.

And then suddenly he pulled away and stepped back. Raking his fingers through his hair, he squeezed his eyes shut.

She worked to steady her trembling limbs, her thundering heart, her weak knees. But it was no use. If he'd been pleased with her kiss, his reaction would have been very different. No guy who was pleased to have been kissed would squeeze his eyes shut.

Oh, lord. What had she done? No matter how much she wanted him, she knew he didn't want her. Yet, she couldn't stop herself from forcing the issue.

Mortification replaced desire. She turned on her heel and raced up the stairs.

The drive to the airport for the trip to North Carolina was made in complete silence. For the better part of the night before, Suzanne had actually considered not going to Maggie and Nick's wedding, but in the end she couldn't stay away. She couldn't turn down the possibility of making friends of Whitney and Maggie. She'd liked them too much to let a little thing like personal humiliation keep her home. God knew, she and Cade had ignored each other for two weeks, they could certainly ignore each other for a three-hour plane ride.

The pilot and copilot said good morning and disappeared into the cockpit to start the engines.

As the plane took off, she put her head back and closed her eyes. She heard the sounds of Cade moving about, then his voice when he said, "Juice?"

Surprised by his consideration, she quietly said, "No. I'm fine."

He opened his juice with a quiet pop. "So are we going to talk about this or what?"

She remembered their last plane ride, how Cade hadn't wanted to talk about what had happened in his den before she told him she was Andreas's Holdings' missing shareholder, and decided to take a page from his book. Rather than face her humiliation, she would simply refuse to discuss it.

Not opening her eyes, she said, "I don't think we have anything to talk about."

"I shouldn't have kissed you—"

Unfortunately, she couldn't let him take the blame. "You didn't kiss me. I kissed you."

"I seem to remember being a party."

That almost made her smile, but she still didn't open her eyes. "Now you're just trying to make me feel better."

"Yeah, I am." He paused, then added, "I can't take you to Nick's house all quiet like this. The women will skin me alive first and ask questions later. We have to deal with this."

For that, she opened her eyes. Sitting in the back, with his boot-covered feet on the desk, Cade didn't look a thing like a billionaire businessman, though he did look like a man prepared to discuss a problem.

But her problem wasn't that they'd kissed again. It was that she was falling in love with him and he didn't want her, so there was no way she would discuss it. And if she'd stop wallowing in her misery he'd probably let her alone. "We're fine."

"Really?"

"Yes."

"Well, it's a long plane ride. If you change your mind, I'm here."

* * *

Cade took his feet off the desk and prepared to work, proud of himself. He might not have gotten her to talk, but he'd made the offer and now they were at least polite enough that they wouldn't raise any suspicions when they got to Nick and Maggie's.

He shouldn't have kissed her the day before, but this time he'd recovered more quickly than he had from the last kiss. He was proud of the fact that he was able to talk to her. To treat her like any other person. To forget she was gorgeous. Toss wanting to sleep with her to the back of his mind. Now, when they arrived at Nick and Maggie's they would be normal.

Still, what pleased him the most was that even after that blistering kiss, he could relegate his sexual feelings for her to the back of his brain and not let them rule him.

He opened a file to get a little work done, but his gaze wandered over to Suzanne. Her eyes were closed, her head back. Her long neck was exposed. Without warning, visions of nibbling that long slim throat filled his brain, his hormones awoke, his body tensed for action.

He banished the visions, subdued his hormones and told his body to settle down. His family considered Suzanne one of theirs. And though he might not have agreed at first, discovering how alone she was, he knew it would be selfish of him to keep her away from Maggie and Whitney when she needed a family. So he could not nibble her neck. Slide his hands along the sleek curve of her waist. Press her into a mattress with the entire length of his body…

He squeezed his eyes shut.

Damn.

Just when he thought he was doing so well.

He leaned back against his seat, mimicking Suzanne. This sexual thing he felt for her wasn't going away. He should have realized that when he couldn't turn away her kiss the day before. Even if he had been able to control himself, and he hadn't, now Suzanne was having trouble controlling her reactions to him. But that was only part of it. He didn't just have a sexual thing for her; he also didn't like to see her sad. He hated the idea of her baby needing a daddy and hated even worse that someday some other guy would be that daddy because that meant someday some other guy would be Suzanne's lover.

So maybe it was time to start thinking of alternatives?

He couldn't marry her. He wouldn't tie another woman to him. But he cared enough about Suzanne and was attracted enough that he knew this wasn't just going to disappear because they wanted it to. He had to fix it, even if it was with only a partial solution.

Carrying Mitzi, Suzanne stood behind Cade as he opened the front door of Nick's house without knocking. They stepped into a foyer that rang with the voices of people in the open-floor-plan family room and kitchen, and she glanced around in awe. The place was much bigger on the inside than it appeared from the outside. Pale orange tile led to a cherrywood staircase that spiraled up three stories, meaning there was plenty of space for family and she didn't have to worry about being too close to Cade.

It was cute that he'd wanted to talk in the plane. But that had only made things worse. He'd made her laugh when she'd wanted to crawl into a hole and die. He cared about her. He was attracted to her and she was attracted to him.

She just plain wanted to be allowed to love him and she wanted him to love her.

And as soon as her mind drifted in that direction, she knew she was in trouble. Luckily, Cade brought her back to reality by shouting, "We're here," as he set their suitcases on the floor beside the tall staircase.

When he didn't get an answer, presumably because he hadn't been heard above the noise coming from the kitchen, he simply left their luggage on the foyer floor and walked into the family room off the kitchen.

"Daddy, you put in too much shrimp!" Maggie stood beside a man who looked to be in his fifties. With his red hair and green eyes so much like Maggie's, it was easy to see he was her father.

"There can never be too much shrimp in jambalaya." Maggie's dad noticed them standing in the door and grinned at them over a huge pot on the six-burner stove in the center island of a pale oak kitchen with black granite countertops. "Hey! Nice to see you, Cade."

"Nice to see you, too, Charlie." He nodded in Suzanne's direction. "This is Suzanne Caldwell and her daughter, Mitzi."

"Your missing shareholder."

Maggie came from behind the stove and hugged Suzanne. "I'm so glad you could come. Let me take Mitzi."

She slid the baby out of Suzanne's arms as Cade motioned to Mr. Forsythe. "This is Maggie's dad, Suzanne, Charlie Forsythe."

"Nice to meet you, kiddo."

"Nice to meet you, too, Mr. Forsythe."

"Everybody calls me Charlie."

Just then the French doors opened. Whitney walked in carrying Maggie's son, Michael. Liz, the nanny, walked in behind her, holding Gino.

"Is that Mitzi?" Whitney cried then she spotted Suzanne. "It is Mitzi!" She raced over and hugged Suzanne. "You're just in time for lunch." She released Suzanne and hugged Cade. "Darius and Nick are on the deck grilling. You might want to join them."

"First, tell me what rooms we're in and I'll take the bags up."

Charlie waved him out the door. "I'll take the bags up. You go see your brothers."

Suzanne followed Charlie as he took her bags upstairs and directed her to a bedroom with a crib and a bathroom. It wasn't a suite, but a simple, comfortable room with access to the gorgeous upstairs deck that looked out over the ocean.

"It's beautiful."

"Yeah, Nick's got good taste," Charlie said, grinning. "Lunch in ten minutes. You don't want to miss my jambalaya." With that he left. Suzanne took a minute to unpack a few things and wash her face before going back downstairs to the noisy kitchen.

Whitney and Maggie immediately bombarded her with questions about the diner. Suzanne answered them, only to be rewarded with another round, until her nervousness disappeared as it had on her weekend in Montauk with these two women. As they set the long table in front of a huge window with a view of the Atlantic, Suzanne remembered thinking that being with

Whitney and Maggie made her feel like she had sisters, and for a few seconds she let herself wonder what it would be like to be part of this big, noisy group.

Considering that only family owned shares of Andreas Holdings, owning one-third of the company did make her family of a sort. As long as she owned her shares, she really was one of them. And maybe in the eighteen months it would take for the brothers to come up with the money to buy her out she really could make friends with Maggie and Whitney—then she'd always be a part of their group.

But even as she thought that, Cade came inside and she knew that wasn't true. Every time he was nice to her, she grew to like him just a little more and pretty soon her feelings might not be so easy to hide. And then what? Every time Maggie or Whitney would invite her somewhere Cade would be there. And some of those times he'd probably have a woman with him. How could he not? He was too gorgeous to be alone. And some women wouldn't want what Suzanne wanted.

They'd settle for a one-night stand or a weekend here or there.…

She nearly gasped. Dear God. What was she thinking? That she should marry him? She'd only known him a few weeks!

But in her heart of hearts she knew she wasn't wrong.

She wanted to marry him. And he wanted nothing to do with her.

CHAPTER TEN

NICK and Maggie's wedding took place at two o'clock Saturday afternoon on the beach right behind Nick's house.

Wearing a white gauze sundress and a big white sun hat, Maggie came out of the beach house and descended the deck stairs. Charlie walked her down a short path to the beach, where—two feet away from waves that crawled ever closer to their flip-flops—Nick, Darius and Cade stood with the minister. All three of them wore cutoff jeans and a T-shirt.

Nick's mom, Becky, a pretty blonde, stood near them. Suzanne and Whitney's parents, a wealthy New York lawyer and his wife, stood behind Becky. To the left, wearing sundresses and floppy sun hats, Whitney and a friend of Maggie's served as bridesmaids. And in front of them was a small group of Maggie's friends and employees from the manufacturing plant she managed for Nick.

It was the oddest wedding Suzanne had ever seen, but she wasn't really experienced with weddings. Most ceremonies she'd attended had been held in churches. Most grooms wore tuxes. Most brides wore a gown. But Nick and Maggie wanted the beach. They wanted to be comfortable. To declare their love.

Just the thought brought tears to Suzanne's eyes. Their love story had been a beautiful one. It was wonderful to see Maggie walk up to Nick, take his hand, declare her love in front of the minister, then cry softly as Nick read the vows he'd written.

Suzanne's tears brimmed over, and her gaze strolled to Cade. He held himself casually, as if he were unaffected by this ceremony, but he wasn't grinning the way Darius was. The way a brother would be. And Suzanne understood why. Darius could be silly and make jokes about Nick losing his freedom because he was with the love of his life, too. Cade had found and lost the love of his life. The memories brought to him by this ceremony were probably bittersweet.

Tilting her head to one side, she studied him, amazed that a woman could inspire that much devotion in a man. But, getting to know his family, she was beginning to understand it. The entire Andreas family was loyal, but Cade was loyal to a fault. If he'd fallen in love it had been forever. For good.

It was part of why she loved him. Even though he hadn't wanted her around, he was good to her. Fairness and honesty weren't just words for him; they were a code to live by. After the way she'd been treated by her friends and Bill Baker, was it any wonder she admired those qualities? Any wonder she admired Cade himself? He was a good man, somebody she *desperately* wanted to love because he embodied all the qualities she would look for in the next man she gave herself to.

Halfway through Nick's vows, Whitney's mom handed a tissue to Suzanne who began crying in earnest when the minister pronounced Nick and Maggie husband and wife. They were a gorgeous couple who would be bountifully happy for the rest of their lives. It was a beautiful thing to experience.

Still, that was only part of the reason she wept. She also wept for Cade. For his loss. For her loss. Because of his past, he'd never want her the way she wanted him, and a man she considered to be just about perfect was lost to her.

She scrambled back to her room, telling Whitney that Mitzi needed a diaper change. She stayed there while Mitzi napped, taking a long bath before she dressed in her red cocktail dress for the semiformal reception being held at a hotel a thirty-minute drive away.

Just before she would have been ready to walk downstairs to join the group, there was a knock at her bedroom door.

Adjusting her grandmother's teardrop pearl earrings, she raced to answer, worried that she was behind schedule and Nick or Maggie had sent someone to get her.

When she opened the door to find Cade, she gaped in amazement. Accustomed to seeing him in jeans and a Stetson, seeing him in a tuxedo rendered her speechless. With his dark, shiny hair combed in a respectable way, he was so good-looking he could have posed for magazine ads.

Praying she wouldn't stutter, she said, "Hey. Am I late?" Then turned around and pressed her hand to her chest. He would tempt a nun out of the convent. So it was not odd or surprising that she was having trouble steadying her breathing and hoping her knees could support her.

"No. I was sent to make sure you knew which limo you were riding in." He ambled into her room. "We're sharing one, by the way."

They were sharing a limo? Lord, she hoped there was another couple or even another person riding with them. Let it be Charlie. Or Whitney's quiet parents.

"I'm ready. I just need to take Mitzi downstairs to Liz."

Cade led her down the spiral staircase. After they deposited Mitzi with the nanny, and Suzanne fussed over her long enough to ease her guilt over leaving, he guided her to the only limo left in front of the house.

She turned around in horror. "I *was* late!"

"Only a bit." He put his hand on the small of her back, where there was no dress, and pin pricks of excitement danced up her spine. "We're fine. Ten minutes behind them at most."

He directed her into the empty limo and her heart galloped. She was so late there was no other couple to ride with them. They were alone! Alone! She was going to make a colossal fool of herself.

She sat on the sofalike seat, shifting over as far as she could, basically hugging the wall.

Rather than sit beside her, Cade sat across from her.

She wrestled back a sigh of relief, not wanting to embarrass herself. But she knew that he knew she'd worked to put space between them.

"Drink?"

"God, no." If she was this nervous and antsy now, imagine what alcohol would do to her. She'd probably drool on him.

The limo pulled out, started off toward the hotel. Suzanne pretended great interest in the scenery.

"Relax. I'm not going to eat you."

She swallowed and tried to laugh. The sound came out strangled.

"Although I have to admit, the first time I saw you in that dress I considered it."

She smiled shakily. "The dress is dramatic. I bought it for the effect."

"Well, you got your money's worth." He leaned back, unbuttoned his jacket and lounged against the seat.

Looking so tempting she could have happily snuggled up to him, he smiled. "You know when you asked me for a few minutes alone that night at the barbecue, I thought you were going to seduce me."

"I know." Dear God, had her voice actually squeaked?

He shook his head. "I had some plans for you that night."

That sent a shaft of heat directly to her womanhood. They had to change the subject or she'd start to shiver. "I saw the look in your eyes. That was why I didn't waste time before I told you about my stock."

He chuckled. The rich, warm sound filled the air around her and seemed to wrap her in the essence of him.

"Yeah, well, if you could have read my mind you probably would have run for the hills." He paused, cocked his head and smiled sexily. "Or maybe not."

After a few seconds' pause, he kicked the toe of her stiletto-heeled sandals and caught her gaze. "You wouldn't have been sorry."

"Now it sounds like you're propositioning me."

He shrugged. "Maybe I am?" He smiled. "We're attracted. And we can't seem to control our chemistry. Or ignore it. Or avoid it. Because we're normal, healthy people. But we're also adults who should be able to discreetly enjoy what's between us."

"I have a baby."

"I have a ranch. What difference does it make?"

"It makes a lot of difference and you know it. I've already told you I want a father for Mitzi."

"And you know I already love Mitzi. You know I would be a good daddy to her for as long as we would be together. We'd just avoid the mess of promises of happily ever after. We both know that doesn't exist. So if we don't get married, just—" he nonchalantly lifted a shoulder "—live together, and you get tired of me and my work schedule, you'd have a get out of jail free card."

"Get out of jail free?"

"You could leave. No hassle. No questions."

She sucked in a quiet breath, not liking his idea. She already knew she was in love with him. She'd never leave. Never. "And what if you got tired?"

He grinned. "Tired? Of making love to you?" He laughed. "I don't think you're going to have to worry about that one."

Just then the limo door opened. Suzanne hadn't even realized they'd stopped moving. Cade stepped out then leaned in again. Offering his hand to help her out, he grinned at her.

She sucked in a breath, urging her heart and lungs to function normally, but the second he grasped her fingers, both her pulse and breathing went haywire again.

He tugged gently and she stepped out of the limo, but she struggled a bit to get her footing and he steadied her with a hand at the small of her back.

Arousal exploded inside her. She fought to suppress a shiver.

He smiled, slowly, knowingly. "See? We'd be very good together. And we'd probably last longer than you think."

"But you don't love me."

"I wouldn't be asking you to live with me if I didn't have feelings for you."

But not love. He didn't say it. He didn't have to. He'd already told her he'd had the love of his life. If she took his offer she'd be second-best. Always second place in his heart and his life. But would that be so bad? They'd be together. He'd help raise Mitzi. She'd be part of his wonderful family.

He said, "Just think about it a bit," before he turned them in the direction of the hotel ballroom.

Nick and Maggie greeted them at the door. Wearing a tux like Cade's, Nick looked almost as handsome as his younger brother. Maggie was breathtaking in a floor-length ivory sheath. It was, after all, their second wedding. She hadn't wanted to wear white or something too youthful. So she'd settled for classy and looked the part of a millionaire's sophisticated wife.

Cade guided her to the table reserved for family. Throughout the meal, Nick's mom, Becky, kept them entertained with stories from Maggie's and Nick's past—especially how they'd loved each other from childhood—until Suzanne's heart swelled with longing. She glanced over at Cade. There was no doubt he was gorgeous. The kind of man who could sweep a woman off her feet in seconds, not even minutes. But the love Becky had described was so pure and so innocent…so perfect, that she knew that was what she wanted—no, it was what she needed.

If she agreed to what Cade was offering, he might always want her sexually but she'd never have the all-consuming, innocent, wonderful love that she wanted. The kind that would steal her breath, wrap her heart in warmth, take her through the rest of her life.

Could she live without it?

With dinner over, the band played a soft romantic song for Nick and Maggie. The way they put their heads together and whispered caused Suzanne's heart to squeeze. They were more than attuned to each other; they were a matching set, two halves to a whole.

And Suzanne had her answer for Cade. She so desperately wanted the kind of closeness Maggie and Nick had. No matter how much she loved Cade, he didn't love her. She couldn't settle for second-best.

When Cade asked her to dance, she rose automatically, but hesitated as they walked to the dance floor. She'd been falling in love with him since the day she met him, but he had not been falling in love with her. With his offer, he'd put all his cards on the table and she had no more excuses, no starry-eyed hopes. She knew what he wanted from her. And it wasn't what she wanted from him.

They reached the dance floor and Cade slid his hand to the small of her back. Tingles formed. Everything female in her responded. To his touch. His scent. His very presence.

He pulled her close and the desire to rest her

head on his shoulder nearly overwhelmed her. So she looked away. Unfortunately she saw Whitney and Darius dancing. Saw the closeness. Saw the intimacy of their glances. The way they danced like people who knew each other's next move long before it was made.

Her heart stuttered.

She wanted that.

She so desperately wanted that. So what was she doing with a man who couldn't give it to her?

"Relax."

She swallowed and looked up into Cade's face. His eyes were bright, alert, like a cat waiting to pounce. She had absolutely no doubt that he desired her. But she couldn't let that muddy the waters. She'd made up her mind. It was time to be strong.

She stepped back. "I think I need some air."

His arms dropped away, but he immediately caught her hand. "There's a patio." He nudged his head in the direction of open French doors. "Come on."

Oh, great. If they were going outside, alone, she might have actually made things worse.

But he didn't seem to notice her hesitation. He led her across the crowded dance floor to a slight breach in the crowd then guided her to doors that opened onto a patio.

She gulped in air as he pulled her along the stone floor to a cobblestone path that wound through a tropical garden. When they'd walked past the reach of the outdoor lights, he stopped.

"Is this air enough for you?" He slid his hands to her back and pulled her close. "I sort of like it out here myself."

She should have told him she'd thought about his offer and had decided to decline. Instead, instinct took over and she leaned in against him. He was solid and warm and very, very real. True, he could never love her, but she did love him. A chance to be with him like this would never come along again. She wanted this minute, this one minute, to at least be held by him.

His hands inched up her spine, along her bare flesh, raising goose bumps. When they reached her shoulders, he pulled her closer still, lowered his head and kissed her.

The bottom dropped out of her world. His lips

moved over hers possessively, taking not asking, because they'd kissed before. Twice.

And she answered just as passionately because if this was her last chance to kiss him she was going to make it good. She might never have seen herself as being assertive, but she had changed. She owned half a business. She had good ideas. And maybe that was the problem. She was no longer the frightened young woman who winced and ran away. She stayed and fought....

Maybe she should be fighting to win him?

He pulled her closer still, bringing her body against his. Even through the folds of his tuxedo jacket she could feel the strong beat of his heart and thrilled to the realization *she* was doing this. His heart was beating for her.

He was everything she wanted. Sexy. Smart. Savvy. Strong.

But that was the kicker. He was strong. Much stronger than she was, even with her newfound confidence. He wouldn't tame easily. If he tamed at all.

And if she didn't step away now, she'd never step away.

With a sigh of regret, she pulled back. "Stop."

He chuckled. "I don't have to. You just did."

She sucked in a breath of air. "Okay. Here's the deal. I like you."

He put his hands on her hips and dragged her back to him. "I like you, too."

She shook her head. "No. I *like* you." She winced. This was not the time to be pussyfooting around. This was the time to be real. Honest. "I *love* you. You might be able to get involved like this." She motioned with her hand between them, indicating their physical relationship. "But I want more."

"That's why we're out here away from everybody."

Panic raced through her. "No. Not *that* more. I mean more as in a relationship, a real relationship, not a tryst in the dark. Not a secret affair." She swallowed. If she was doing this, she had to go the whole way. "I want you to love me."

His hands fell to his sides. "Oh?"

She squeezed her eyes shut as disappointment flooded her. Deep down inside she'd almost hoped he'd say he did love her or, at the very least, that he believed that someday he could love her. Instead, he'd confirmed her worst suspicions. He wasn't interested in love. Only sex.

She licked her lips, savoring the taste of him, a taste she'd never get again, and stepped back. "Come on, Cade. I've been saying it all along. I have a child. I need a home. A real home. I'm just starting to build my life again and I want to do it right."

"And living with me would be wrong."

"What Whiskey Springs man in his right mind would ever approach me after we'd lived together? You employ nearly everyone. I'd be a pariah."

He combed his fingers through his hair as if he knew she was right.

She shook her head sadly. "Did you think we could live together for a few months or maybe even years with no consequences?"

"I don't know."

"There'd be consequences. They are always consequences." Like her currently shattering heart that still, God help her, held on to the hope that he wouldn't let her go.

He put another two feet of distance between them. "I get it."

And by the fact that he'd taken another step back, she knew that he did understand. He wouldn't argue and give her false hope or make promises he couldn't keep.

She turned and walked away. Up the garden path alone.

Pain rolled through her in a trembling wave. Her throat closed. Still, she fought the tears. She had at least another hour of this reception and there was no way she'd let anybody know Cade had broken her heart.

She was done being the person everybody pitied. She'd do her crying in private.

She rode home in a limo with Darius and Whitney, silently packed her things and ordered a cab that took her to the airport, where she used her one-and-only credit card to get a commercial flight. She found a late flight and climbed aboard the nearly empty plane. When she arrived in Texas, she called Amanda Mae to pick her up and by noon next day, she was at Cade's gathering the last of her few belongings.

"So what are you going to do?"

Having already cried herself out on the dark plane, she shrugged. "Not sure."

"Where are you going to go?"

Longing for her grandmother tightened her chest, brought tears to her eyes again. "I think I'd like to visit my gram."

Amanda Mae frowned. "Oh, honey, you're sad enough. Don't go to the cemetery."

"No. No cemetery. I thought I'd spend some time outside our old house. Just soak myself in the memory of what it felt like to be loved."

"If you don't stop, you're going to make me cry."

"I just need a little bit of something to hold on to. I came here looking for a job and found friends." She squeezed Amanda Mae's hand. "But I think I might have let go of my past too soon."

"Because it sucked."

She laughed in spite of herself. "No. It's more than that. I was so wrapped up in meetings with lawyers and accountants that I never really mourned my gram." She sat on the bed beside her friend. "I wonder now if that wasn't part of why I was so quick to fall for Cade. So quick to see him as a husband. A daddy."

Amanda Mae squeezed her hand. "You saw what he is. A good man. Don't fault yourself. Fault him. He's the one who can't move on."

And with that, they left her suite, her pathetic suitcase in Amanda Mae's hand, Mitzi in her carrier. They said goodbye on the driveway of Cade's big house and Suzanne promised she'd be back soon. But she didn't think she would be. She'd rather entice Amanda Mae to visit in Georgia. Maybe start a bigger diner. Or a bakery. Or anything Suzanne wanted because in another seventeen months she'd be a very wealthy woman.

Still a sad woman…but a very wealthy one.

CHAPTER ELEVEN

MONDAY morning, Cade headed for the stables, resisting the urge to drive to town to check on Suzanne to make sure she was okay. He'd gotten the skinny from his staff that Amanda Mae had brought Suzanne home and they'd packed up her belongings. He knew she'd probably gone to Amanda Mae's to live. Which was fine. Probably for the best.

He'd made a fool of himself with her. He thanked his lucky stars no one had been within hearing distance in that garden at Nick's wedding because his foolishness was only his own personal embarrassment.

Oh, he got what she was saying. She wanted what he didn't. Marriage. But the real underlying sentiment was much simpler. She wanted him to love her, and he simply couldn't risk it.

So he'd let her walk away, let her go back to Nick's beach house in the limo with Darius and Whitney. When she wasn't around on Sunday afternoon he'd correctly assumed she'd taken a commercial flight back to Texas.

He stopped his truck in front of the main stable and jumped out.

Standing with one foot hooked over the fence and his black Stetson shielding his eyes from the sun, Jim greeted him. "Hey, Cade. How was the wedding?"

"Great." That wasn't exactly a lie, but he certainly wasn't going to tell his father-in-law that he'd propositioned Suzanne and she'd rejected him. "Nick's house at the beach is a paradise. And it's always fun to jag around with my brothers, make 'em feel like losers for settling down."

Jim laughed.

Cade relaxed and continued on into the stable. This was what he needed. Not just a quiet trot around the ranch to check things out, but a little time with Ashley's dad to remind himself that he was doing the right thing by stepping away from Suzanne.

He pulled a saddle from the hook on the wall as Jim said, "Heard that little girl from Georgia went with you."

His face heated but he kept walking toward his Appaloosa. "I couldn't exactly leave a house-guest alone while I went off gallivanting. Besides, Maggie and Nick wanted her there."

"She's a pretty little thing."

"I hadn't noticed."

"So what's this? You blind now?"

Cade laughed. "All right. She's pretty. But you know I'm not interested."

Jim opened the corral door. "Cade, it's been *years.*"

"Two. Hey, Sugar," he crooned, approaching his horse. "I think you and I need to spend a little quality time together." Sugar lifted his head and whinnied. Cade grunted as he hoisted the saddle to his horse's back.

"Two long years," Jim said, helping Cade cinch the saddle.

"What? You think I have no concept of the passage of time?"

"I'm just saying it seems odd is all. We all loved

Ashley. Her mom and I talk about her every day. But you're young. You should be moving on."

"I have moved on. Hell, I've got more work now than I ever had. And more people depending on me." Which was what he wanted—association with people but from a distance. This way he didn't hurt anyone.

He led Sugar out of the stable and spent the afternoon riding the fence until it ended, and just plain exploring the land beyond that.

Now both Ashley and Suzanne were gone. And he would have to deal with it.

That night Cade didn't sleep. He went to his office where he spent hours poring over reports for the new division of his oil conglomerate, even though he didn't absorb a word he read. At seven Eric arrived, took one look and simply headed into his office without comment.

But two days later, when he still hadn't slept, Jim wasn't as polite as Eric. "You look like hell."

"I haven't been sleeping."

"Word got back from town that your little girl

from Georgia hasn't been showing up at the sandwich stand."

His heart stopped. He'd thought she'd gone to
Amanda Mae's, maybe slept on her couch. He'd
thought she was working the stand, surrounded
by people who were growing to like her. "Her
choice."

"So where'd she go?"

"She didn't tell me."

Jim sighed, fell to a chair in front of Cade's
desk. "Are you slow or are you just plain crazy?"

"What I am is tired. Say what you came in here
to say then leave."

To his surprise, Jim rose from his chair and
walked to the door that separated Cade's office
from Eric's. He closed it.

"Okay, I'll say my piece then I'll be gone.
Suzanne was a cute little gal with a heart of gold
and a very good head on her shoulders. And you
liked her. Maybe even loved her. Yet you chased
her away."

"I did not love her!"

"Really? You're not eating. You're not sleeping.

You didn't even behave this badly when Ashley died."

The reality of that hit Cade like a punch to the chest. He couldn't sleep. He couldn't eat. He couldn't even work. Even after Ashley died, he could work.

"Oh, God." He pressed his fingers to his eyes. He did love her. "This is so wrong."

"How can you say that?"

"Because I wasn't a very good husband to the last woman I married." He sucked in a breath. "You know as well as I do that I left her alone. Lots. It hurt her."

Jim shook his head. "You were building a business. She always understood. Besides, you were there when it counted most."

Jim might believe that but Cade didn't. He put a business deal ahead of his dying wife. He wasn't around when she drew her last breath. The very second she needed him the most, he was gone.

"Cade?"

"I don't want to talk about it."

"This is about you not being there when she died, isn't it?"

He said nothing.

"Oh, Cade. She'd rebounded. That morning she was happy as a lark. As I recall, she shooed you out. Because you'd been there every day for weeks." He sucked in a breath. "How can you not remember this? How can you not remember the vacations? The long weekends? The days when you only owned stocks and the ranch…when every other day was a holiday for you?"

Cade swallowed. Every time he thought of his marriage, he only remembered himself leaving. He remembered all the times he wasn't home as if they ran in a long unbroken stream. He'd forgotten the weeks he'd been able to take long vacations with Ashley because he worked for himself. He'd forgotten the days he'd stayed home just because he could. He'd forgotten the two weeks before she died, when he hadn't left her side, when he'd slept on a couch by the hospital bed they'd set up in a room near the kitchen.

When Cade said nothing, Jim tossed up his hands in defeat. "All I'm saying is you're a fool to let a good woman walk away. A fool not to take a second chance when the good Lord decides to give you one."

He rose and headed for the door. "That's it. That's my piece. I said it. What you do with it is your business."

The first night after Suzanne left Whiskey Springs, she'd gotten a hotel room for herself and Mitzi. The second night, having arrived in Georgia, she got another hotel room and bought some newspapers so she could begin house hunting.

But the third night, even in the familiar hotel room, she felt alone and cold. So lonely she could have happily curled in a ball and cried for hours. But she didn't. She couldn't. She had a child.

So she called Amanda Mae. "Hey."

"Hey. It's pretty damned late to be calling a woman who has to get up at five to make your cinnamon roll recipe."

"Sorry about that."

"I hate making those blasted things. Can't I persuade you to come home?"

Home. Whiskey Springs had become home, but

she'd made the mistake of falling for Cade and she couldn't live there anymore. "I thought you said you were fine on your own."

"I thought I would be, but I'm not. I'm used to your company. Can't we just ban Cade from the diner when it opens next week?"

Just the thought made Suzanne laugh. Still, she didn't want to talk about Cade. Every time she even thought of him, her chest hurt. Her eyes filled with tears.

"You visit your gram yet?"

She sucked in a breath. "No. Maybe tomorrow. I'll sit outside the gates, look at the house, remember some things."

"Makes sense. Just don't stay too long or think too much."

"I won't." Because things were getting too sentimental, she changed the subject. "Amanda Mae, I think it's finally sinking in that in eighteen months I'm going to be rich."

"I know."

"And I have to figure out how to manage that money so I don't lose most of it the way my grandmother did."

"Personally, I don't think you should have sold the stock. You should have waited around for the company to rebound and then been a real thorn in the Andreas brothers' sides."

Suzanne laughed in spite of the pain that crushed her heart when she thought of the Andreas brothers, their wives, their babies. People who should have been her friends. They were lost to her now. "I don't want to be anything to them."

"Of course you do. I think that's the problem. You'd be part of their family if that stubborn old mule Cade wasn't such an idiot."

Suzanne smiled at the motherly tone in Amanda Mae's voice, even as the tears in her eyes spilled over. This time she didn't try to stop them. Mitzi was finally asleep so she wouldn't hear. And maybe a good cry was what she needed to get herself out of this maudlin mood?

"Look. I've gotta go. I'm really tired."

Amanda Mae sighed. "I should take a piece of that boy's hide."

"No. Let it go, Amanda Mae."

Suzanne clicked off, but Amanda Mae's eyes narrowed. Everybody in this town kowtowed to

Cade Andreas, but Amanda Mae Fisher had long ago realized a woman had to fight for what she wanted.

She shrugged off her robe and threw it to her bed before she put on blue jeans and a T-shirt. It might be late, but she was mad.

When his doorbell rang after eleven, Cade cursed. He stormed up the hall, thinking the blooming idiot ringing his bell would wake Mitzi. Then he remembered Mitzi no longer lived with him. Sadness seeped into his soul, but he stopped it. Regardless of what his father-in-law thought, he couldn't get over leaving Ashley the day she died. Couldn't drag Suzanne into his life when his past relationship had been such a disaster.

He yanked open the door only to find an angry Amanda Mae Fisher on his front step.

"You are a freaking pain in my butt."

Cade stifled a long-suffering sigh. "Look, I know you're miffed. I know you want your partner back but—"

"I don't give a flying fig about having a partner. I ran that diner alone for fifteen years. I can run it alone another fifteen. But I do miss my friend." She stopped, sucked in a breath. "Cade, you know I haven't got any kids. And she was like my kid. In here—" she patted the spot where her heart would be "—I felt a connection. You know what it's like to be alone. Why would you force me to live without the chance to be somebody's mama, even if it is unofficial?"

Cade squeezed his eyes shut then popped them open again. Everybody was blaming him for Suzanne leaving, but it had been her choice. And didn't anybody see he was suffering, too?

"I don't know what you want me to do—"

"Go after her," Amanda Mae said, not giving him a chance to make any of his excuses. "It's you she wants. Sometime tomorrow she's going back to the estate she shared with her gram. She can't get inside, but she intends to spend some time sitting outside the gates, thinking about her past, remembering her gram. That poor kid's been through enough. Don't let her go on suffering just because you think you don't want her here."

The truth of that hurt his heart. He did want her

here. He did love her. He'd realized that talking to Jim. But things between him and Suzanne were not as simple or cut-and-dried as Jim or Amanda Mae thought.

He'd had a great love and he hadn't been there for her when she needed him the most. Despite Jim's kind reassurances that haunted him. Hurt him. Held him back. Who was he to get a second chance at love?

He didn't deserve it and Suzanne deserved better.

Cade went to bed that night feeling cold and lonely. He crawled under the covers of the big bed that had been his and Ashley's, the only thing he'd brought from the master suite into his new room after her death.

Because he hadn't been able to sleep since Suzanne had gone, he didn't think he'd sleep that night, either. But he laid his head on the pillow and didn't have another thought. He immediately drifted off.

But it was a fitful sleep. A sleep filled with worry for Suzanne. He didn't know how much money she'd spent on the diner. How much money she had left. He hoped she'd have enough for a house but what if she didn't? What if she could only afford to rent a shabby apartment in a run-down section of the city? She'd be in an area potentially filled with drugs and gangs. And it would be his fault. His brothers would kill him. His sisters-in-law would skin him alive when they found out.

In his dreams they yelled at him. In his dreams, he didn't blame them. He worried about her. Feared for her. Chastised himself.

Then suddenly he was on his Appaloosa, riding. The wind billowed around him. Sun beat down on him. He knew the dream, knew that Ashley waited on the other side of this ride.

He gently nudged Sugar, urging him on.

As he approached the corral, he could see Ashley tending the flowers. He wouldn't get to talk to her. He wouldn't get much more than a few seconds to see her, still he nudged Sugar to go faster.

At the corral, he slid off the horse and stopped. He raised his hand to wave the way he always did, and this time he didn't feel the silk pillow case. He didn't awaken.

Joy trembled through him.

"Ashley?"

She turned and smiled. His heart tripped over itself.

"Cade."

The sound of her voice was nearly his undoing. Joy and sorrow buffeted him like a ray of sunlight and an angry wind. He wanted to see her, talk to her, but he knew he didn't deserve it.

He took two steps over, but stopped, worried that if he got too close she'd vanish.

She smiled again, a warm, gentle smile that reminded him of just how young she was. How young she'd been when they'd married. How shy. How timid. By now, Suzanne would have come over, asked him a million questions. Maybe even kissed him. Ashley stayed where she was.

He swallowed. There was a gulf between them. Not just distance. Not even life and death. A real gulf. He knew her. He loved her. But not the way he knew Suzanne. Not the way he loved Suzanne.

She smiled again. Her head tilted to the side

as if she were studying him, figuring something out. Then she raised her hand and waved slightly. "Goodbye, Cade."

Tears filled his eyes. "No." He stopped. He couldn't keep her. He knew he couldn't keep her. He swallowed once. Then whispered, "Goodbye, Ash."

When he woke, his room was totally silent. His weary body was relaxed. His weary mind sharp, alert.

He'd finally gotten to say goodbye.

The next morning, Suzanne awoke determined to find somewhere to live. Hotel rooms weren't cheap and, though she had money, she knew she couldn't stay in a hotel room forever. She wanted a house.

She woke Mitzi, fed her, bathed her and dressed her for the day. After checking out of the hotel, she took her meager possessions, mostly secondhand things she'd bought while in Whiskey Springs, and drove to a department store.

In a few months, she'd be filthy rich. She

wouldn't squander what she had but, by God, she and Mitzi could at least not look like refugees.

In the store, she bought clothes for Mitzi, a stroller, a walker and two teddy bears. She bought shirts and jeans, shorts, skirts, tennis shoes and flat sandals for herself. And some makeup. She even found a salon and was lucky enough to get a walk-in appointment to have her hair trimmed.

With her hair coiffed, she asked for directions to the ladies' room and changed into a stylish skirt with a ruffled blouse very much like the one Whitney had worn the day she met her. As fascinated Mitzi watched, she put on makeup, fluffed out her hair and headed out to the parking lot.

Her Mercedes sat waiting. She stuffed all the bags she'd hung on the handles of Mitzi's new stroller into the trunk. Then she buckled Mitzi into her car seat.

Her intention had been to head for a real estate office to begin her search for a house, but when she reached a familiar off-ramp for the Interstate, she took it. She'd told Amanda Mae she wanted to say goodbye to her gram. And this morning she would.

Three turns got her on the road to her grandmother's estate and twenty minutes later, she sat in front of the locked wrought-iron gate, staring at it.

She missed her grandmother. In all the hubbub of straightening out Martha Caldwell's beleaguered estate, she hadn't taken the time to grieve her loss. Looking past the gate to the big house beyond the long, well-tended lawn and flower beds, she couldn't actually see the small front stoop, but she could picture her grandmother sitting on the rocker beside the front door.

She snorted a laugh as tears filled her eyes. Her grandmother loved her front porch rocker, even though she was too far from the street to see anybody or for anybody to see her.

God, she was alone again. And she didn't want to be. She also didn't want to live in Georgia. She wanted to live in Whiskey Springs.

A soft tap on her window brought her out of her haze. She glanced over to see Cade. She didn't know how he'd known where she'd be, but he had. Joy filled her, then sadness. He might have found her, but she guessed Amanda Mae had sent him because he'd made it perfectly clear that he didn't want her.

She wasn't going back to the town where the true love of her life lived…especially since he didn't want her.

"Open the window."

"Go home, Cade."

"I can't go home. Amanda Mae has murder in her eyes. She blames me for you leaving."

Since she couldn't argue that. She didn't. She stared straight ahead.

He groaned noisily. "Come on."

She refused to even look at him.

"Please. We need to talk."

She still stared straight ahead.

"I talked with Ashley last night."

One of her eyebrows rose. Her curiosity was piqued.

Given that Ashley was no longer with them, at the very least, this would be a good story.

With a sigh, she opened her car door. He stepped aside and let her out.

"We had a busy morning. Mitzi's sleeping. I don't want to wake her."

She closed the door softly and faced him. Bad move. Not just because every hormone in her body sprang to aching life. But because he looked awful. Instead of his usual T-shirt and jeans, he wore pleated pants and a dress shirt. He had no hat so his hair blew in the slight breeze created by the overhang of rich green trees that surrounded her grandmother's property. His eyes were dull. Listless.

Talking to a ghost must not be pleasant.

"So?"

He peered over at her. "So?"

"How does a man talk to a wife who passed away?"

He winced. "I had a dream."

Her eyebrows rose.

"You don't understand." He swallowed. "Ever since Ashley died, I'd have this dream. In the beginning, I had it every day, then every week, then once a month."

She said nothing, only studied him. Birds chirped on the quiet street. A rare car drove by, forcing them to step off the road and to the sidewalk.

"I had the dream again last night. And this morning I realized I hadn't had the dream the entire time you were in town."

"Oh?"

He forked his fingers through his hair. "And last night the dream was different. I got to talk to her."

Gazing at her grandmother's house, a wave of empathy for him washed through her. What she wouldn't give for ten minutes with her gram. Just ten minutes to be able to say I love you and maybe hear the words again herself.

"Every time I have the dream, I walk over to her, hoping to say hello." He cleared his throat. "Hoping to get to say goodbye."

Her senses perked up. Things about his grief began to fall into place for her. "You never said goodbye, did you?"

He turned to her, his eyes flashing. "Don't feel sorry for me. I traded the chance to say goodbye for a business deal."

"No, you didn't. At least not on purpose. There

was no way you could have known she would die that day."

He dragged in a breath. "She'd rebounded. She was happy. She shooed me off, saying I needed to get out of the house."

"Sounds to me like she was a really great wife." She shook her head. "Also sounds like you were around a little more than you thought."

"Maybe. Jim says I was. But I'm still something of a workaholic."

She laughed, stepped closer, put her hands on his shoulders to comfort him. She knew none of this had been easy for him. And the important thing was he'd come after her. "You could always change. A person who has billions of dollars doesn't have to work 24/7. He could take a day or a week or maybe even a few months off now and again."

He laughed, draped his hands around her waist. "Maybe." He swallowed. "I used to. Jim sort of reminded me of that, too."

She smiled softly, stepped closer. He felt so good, so strong, so real. "Maybe? There doesn't have to be a debate about it. You should just say yes." She shook her head. "You are a bit of a stubborn mule."

"So Amanda Mae says."

"You're also high-handed. Bossy. Arrogant."

"You think you can handle me?"

She laughed. "I left you, didn't I?"

His hands suddenly lifted from her waist. Slid up her back. Fell down again. "Yes. You did."

"I'm not sorry."

He laughed. "I didn't expect you would be."

"But I am coming back to Whiskey Springs." She peeked at him. "I like owning the diner. I like having my own things. A place in the world."

"I thought you wanted a place with me."

"I thought you didn't want me."

He leaned in, bumped his forehead to hers. "I do."

"You do what?"

"I do want you around."

"Are you asking me to live in sin?"

His head snapped up. His eyes narrowed. "You'd forgive me that easily?"

"Depends on what you say next."

He laughed, yanked her against him. "You're

a smart, sassy, sometimes bossy woman who I think I love."

"Think?"

"Who I definitely love. I don't think I can live without you." He frowned. "No. I don't want to live without you."

Her chest tightened. It amazed her that he recognized the nuance of difference in those two statements. He was choosing her. Not being forced or compelled to love her. But choosing to.

A light, airy feeling invaded her.

"You've gotta say the words, Cade."

He brought her a tad closer. "What words?"

"Fooling around will not get you what you want."

"Fooling around is what I want."

She laughed. "Say the words."

He sobered. "I love you. I do. I want to raise your daughter have six more kids—"

"*Six?*"

"Maybe seven."

Realizing he was giddy, she laughed. "Amanda Mae will shoot me."

"Only if you force her to be the one to bake the

cinnamon rolls every morning." He paused, but only slightly. "Marry me?"

Her eyes filled with tears. "Really? You don't want an adjustment period."

"I hear it takes over a year to plan a wedding these days."

"It does, if you want to do it right."

"I want to do it right."

She pressed her lips together as the tears in her eyes spilled over. "So do I."

Then he kissed her.

EPILOGUE

DARIUS had married Whitney in the ballroom in the mansion of the Andreas family estate on Montauk. Suzanne had seen pictures of the elaborate, but quiet, event. Nick had married Maggie on the beach. She'd been there with them. She'd seen the sandals. Raised an eyebrow over the cutoff jeans Nick had worn.

So it seemed only fitting in Suzanne's eyes that she and Cade have a big church wedding, with a minister, Nick and Darius as groomsmen, Whitney and Maggie as bridesmaids and Gino as ring bearer.

In the bride's room of the huge old gray-stone church that looked more like a cathedral with its vaulted ceilings and regal pillars, Whitney fussed with Suzanne's hair while Maggie straightened the long train of her frilly white gown.

Suzanne sucked in a breath. "How's Liz holding up?" There were four kids now. Three-year-old Gino and toddlers Michael and Mitzi. Plus a baby, since Whitney had given birth to Elizabeth. Dressed in a tiny tux, Gino sat on a fancy Queen Anne chair, his little legs swinging, the pillow for the rings sitting on the counter beside him. But Liz still had three kids to watch until the formal ceremony was over.

"She's fine. She's got plenty of help from Mrs. Reynolds and Mrs. Granger. Cade's den looks like a day care. I'm sure they're having a high old time. Stop fretting!"

She pressed a hand to her stomach. "I can't help it."

Maggie eyed her shrewdly. "Nerves or cold feet?"

"Just nerves."

Whitney laughed. "Afraid of marrying a multi-billionaire?"

She groaned. "I'm more afraid of marrying somebody so good-looking every woman in the world is going to try to steal him."

Maggie chuckled merrily. "Right. Cade only has eyes for you."

As if to confirm that, Cade caught Suzanne's gaze the second she and Marty Higgins stepped into the doorway of the big church and the organist began the chords of "Here Comes the Bride." A longtime friend of Cade's, constant diner customer and now the man dating Amanda Mae, Marty had volunteered to walk Suzanne down the aisle. His request for the honor had been every bit as sweet and sincere as Cade's proposal.

But at this second, she only saw Cade. As her designer gown swished softly on the silk runner that led her to the altar, she held his gaze, loving the way his eyes first skimmed her possessively, then softened with love when they locked with hers.

As she neared the end of the aisle, she looked over at Amanda Mae just in time to see her sobbing into a dainty pink hankie. She glanced at Jim and Audra Malloy and Jim winked at her, a private, special signal and she smiled, then she looked at Ginny, who sat in the seat in front of Jim and Audra. Ginny flashed her a grin before she too burst into tears. Audra Malloy tapped her on the shoulder and handed her a pristine white handkerchief. Sniffing softly, Ginny took it.

Suzanne finished her walk, nervously taking the hand Cade extended. The preacher opened his book and said, "Who gives this woman to be married?"

Marty choked out, "I do," then bussed a kiss across her cheek before he turned and took his seat with Amanda Mae.

She swallowed back her own tears. She'd entered this town a homeless orphan, a woman with no family, no friends. Now, almost one year to the date, she had a partner who acted more like a mom than a business associate. She had two best friends in Maggie and Whitney, and Nick and Darius, who would become real family when she married Cade.

Cade. The love of her life. Her reason to breathe. Her life partner. The man who'd given her a family and who would soon give her more children. Their house would be a noisy, happy place.

She couldn't ask for anything more.

No woman could.

* * * * *

Mills & Boon® Large Print

November 2011

THE MARRIAGE BETRAYAL
Lynne Graham

THE ICE PRINCE
Sandra Marton

DOUKAKIS'S APPRENTICE
Sarah Morgan

SURRENDER TO THE PAST
Carole Mortimer

HER OUTBACK COMMANDER
Margaret Way

A KISS TO SEAL THE DEAL
Nikki Logan

BABY ON THE RANCH
Susan Meier

GIRL IN A VINTAGE DRESS
Nicola Marsh

Mills & Boon® Large Print
December 2011

BRIDE FOR REAL
Lynne Graham

FROM DIRT TO DIAMONDS
Julia James

THE THORN IN HIS SIDE
Kim Lawrence

FIANCÉE FOR ONE NIGHT
Trish Morey

AUSTRALIA'S MAVERICK MILLIONAIRE
Margaret Way

RESCUED BY THE BROODING TYCOON
Lucy Gordon

SWEPT OFF HER STILETTOS
Fiona Harper

MR RIGHT THERE ALL ALONG
Jackie Braun

Mills & Boon® Online

Discover more romance at
www.millsandboon.co.uk

- **FREE** online reads
- **Books** up to one month before shops
- **Browse our books** before you buy

...and much more!

For exclusive competitions and instant updates:

 Like us on **facebook.com/romancehq**

 Follow us on **twitter.com/millsandboonuk**

 Join us on **community.millsandboon.co.uk**

Visit us Online Sign up for our FREE eNewsletter at
www.millsandboon.co.uk